novella one

monday knights

enemy
KISSES

DEBRA ST JAMES

Enemy Kisses

MONDAY KNIGHTS — NOVELLA ONE

DEBRA ST JAMES

Enemy Kisses | Monday Knights — Novella One

© 2023 by Debra St James

Website: www.debrastjamesbooks.com

Email: debrastjamesbooks@gmail.com

Published by: Debra St James Author

Edited by: Cruel Ink Editing and Design

Formatted by: Debra St James Author

ISBN: 978-0-6457395-8-9 [Paperback]

ISBN: 978-0-6457395-9-6 [Discreet Edition Paperback]

ISBN: 978-0-6457395-7-2 [Ebook]

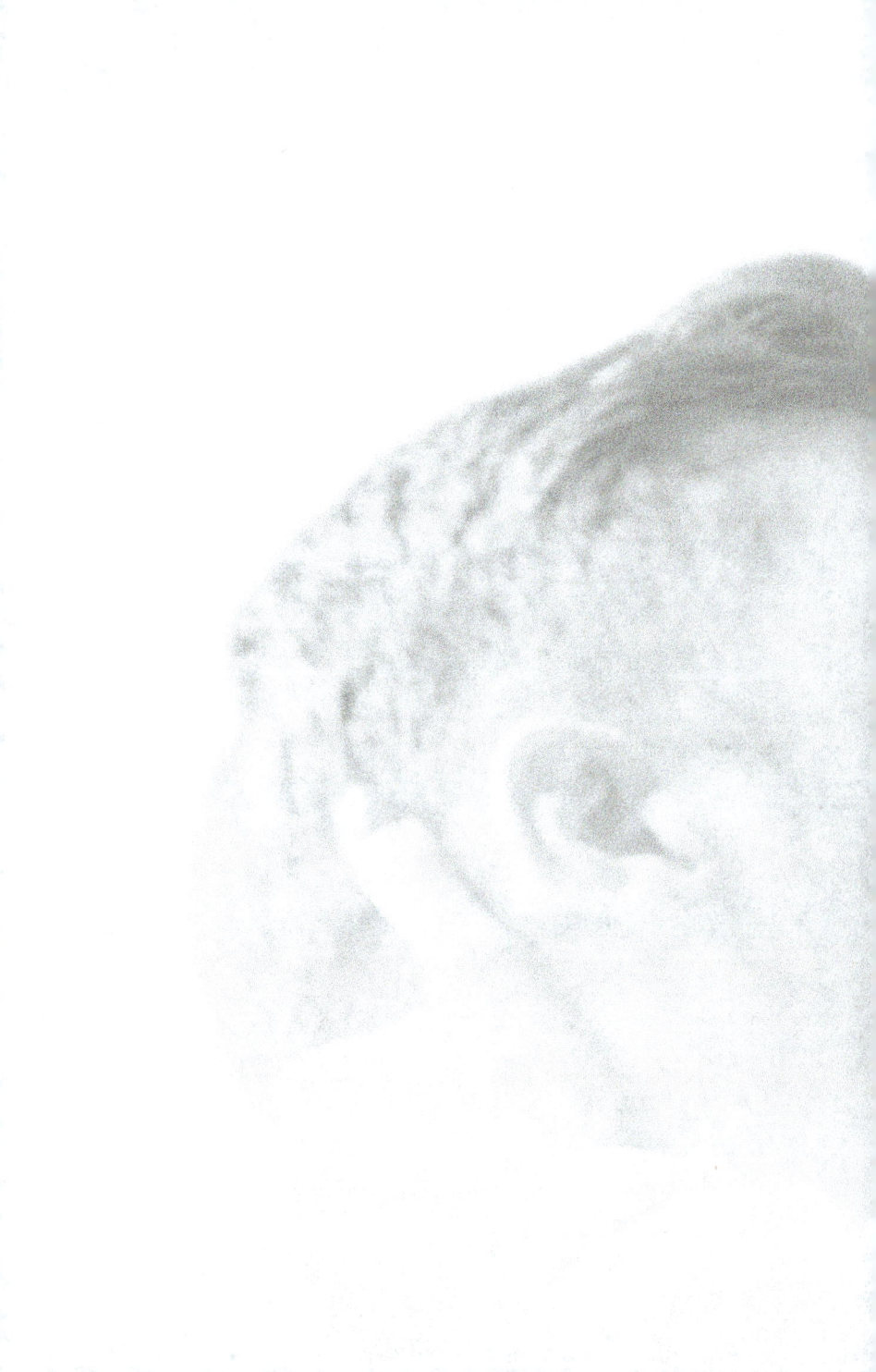

inspiration

This story was inspired by the lyrics ...

—> *Mystify Me by INXS* <—

playlist

Mystify … *INXS*
Cruel to be Kind … *Nick Lowe*
We Can Get Together … *Flowers*
Need You Tonight … *INXS*
Pash … *Kate Ceberano*
Cream … *Prince*
Burn For You … *INXS*

You can check it out here:
https://tinyurl.com/enemykisses-spotify

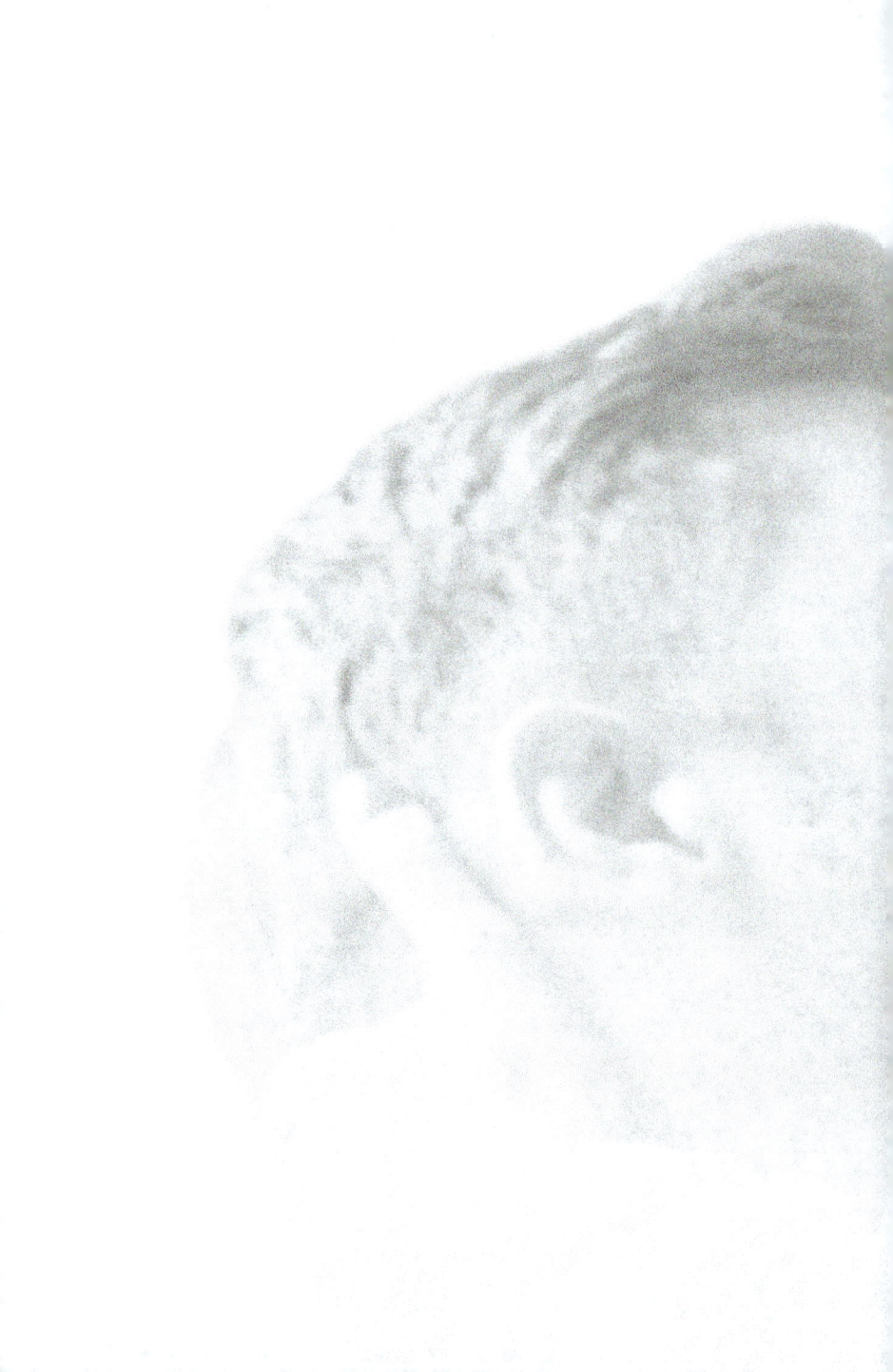

CHAPTER 1

—harriet—

HARRY'S HOUSE OF CRÊPES AND CROISSANTS HAS BEEN OPEN FOR one month today—yay! Go me!

My parents didn't believe I could follow my dream of opening a café, let alone keep one open.

What would they know, anyway?

They were barely around when I was growing up—too busy traveling with Dad's job to raise me—leaving Grand-Mère to do it. She always knew me best and passed on her love of French baking, which she learned from her mother back in France when she was a girl. She also dreamed of opening a café, which inspired me. She taught me everything I know, so I'm bound and determined to prove them wrong and make Grand-Mère proud.

Just thinking about showing them what I'm capable of lights a fire inside me as I make the short bicycle ride from my apartment to my favorite place to be as the barest sliver of orange fights to take over the midnight sky. Besides, I have to make this work because I've used my entire inheritance from Grand-Mère as well as all of my savings to do it. I glance upward and whisper, "Love you, Grand-Mère Mae."

I pedal into the lot behind my café and lock my bike to the fence. *Ugh!* A sour stench infiltrates my nose before I even see the state of the area outside the back door to my brand-new café.

Almost every freaking day, this is what greets me. What's worse is, before I realized what it was, I stepped in the disgusting mess. At least I haven't done that for a few weeks now. But I'm tired of starting my day like this. It's ruining my dream. In all of my imaginings, I never imagined having to step over vomit to enter my building daily. Not only that, but the trash, which is left strewn halfway down the sidewalk and behind my café because of late-night drunken antics, is shameful. And let's not forget to mention the smell of urine along the side of my building and at the front door. All of these misfortunes are directly caused by that damn pub next door. With a huff, I toss the evil eye over my shoulder at the building—like the building itself is to blame for what's happening—glaring at the painted sign that says, *Brady's Pub*. It's like the owner doesn't give a shit about any other businesses around them.

I've had enough. I'm going to give the owner a piece of my mind. Every time I've gone over there to have a civil conversation with the owner, he's not available or hasn't yet arrived for work. I guess he starts late because the bar is open late, whereas I need to be here early to prep for the day. Our schedules couldn't be more opposite, but I've decided to send him an email with photographic evidence of his patrons' misdeeds. I have his email address sitting on my phone, ready to go, and I've had plenty of time to draft what I'm going to say in my head.

Using my phone, I snap a quick photo of today's mess to add to my evidence folder. The pictures should get the message across loud and clear. He won't be able to dispute it.

I unlock the door, careful to step over the foul mess using the light on my phone. Once I'm inside, I flick the switch for the kitchen light, which also illuminates a small area of the back stoop, grab the kitty litter—an added expense I never thought I'd have—and sprinkle a generous amount over the vomit, gagging while I work. People are gross. I leave the litter to do its job, spend half an hour collecting trash—all the while cursing under my breath as I stomp my way around the area out the back—wash my hands thoroughly, turn on the ovens, then grab everything I need to start today's prep.

I flick my eyes up to the clock. Damn it, I'm running late now. I'm going to need to catch up on lost time somehow. Perhaps I should start coming in earlier to account for the time I need to clean up—*ugh*.

"Not again." Quentin's gruff voice breaks the silence as he steps inside.

"Yep. *Again*. It's pretty bad today. I'm guessing it's worse because of the holiday yesterday. And you should have seen all the trash. I haven't been out front yet, but I'm sure it's just as bad."

"Something needs to be done. It's fucking unsanitary."

"I know. I plan to write an email today and attach the photos I've taken. I've had enough."

Quentin grunts, then grabs the broom, sweeping the mess at the back door and disposing of it for me. Then he grabs the disinfectant and scrubs it clean. Such an angel.

"You know what today is?" Quentin studies me closely, then shakes his head. "It's our one-month anniversary. We've been open for one entire month!" I sing.

His lips twitch as he rolls his eyes at me. He thinks he has everyone fooled with his grumpy demeanor, but I know the real person beneath the gruff exterior. He's a soft teddy bear at heart, which comes out in the delicate croissants he makes. The guy has muscles and is covered in tattoos, but you should see him lovingly folding and rolling the delicious, buttery pastries he makes. His creations are to die for—literally.

I remember when I first interviewed him for the position. I was skeptical until he pulled out a box with a variety of croissants he'd prepared for the interview. The buttery texture and crisp, flaky pastry sold me, and I offered him the position on the spot. Another wonderful thing about Quentin is that he comes with Judy, his sweet wife. They were a godsend throughout the renovations, happily volunteering to help with painting and decorating in their free time. I lucked out with them.

I get to work measuring and mixing the batter I'll need to make crêpes throughout the day. I ensure all of my sweet and savory toppings are prepared and transfer the ingredients to the refrigerator out front for easy access.

Judy breezes in from the kitchen, her blonde ponytail bouncing behind her. "Morning!"

"Oh my gosh, is it that time already?"

She chuckles. "Yep. I'll get the tables set up outside." The click of the front door lock sounds as I head back through to the kitchen. Quentin's busy decorating the almond croissants with almond flakes, so I pull out the fillings for our plain croissants, ready to make a handful of each type for our display cabinet out front.

"Cheese and crackers. Have you seen the mess out front?" Judy huffs as she makes her way toward the supply cupboard.

"Nope. Too busy, but if it's anything like it was out back this morning, it'll be pretty bad."

"It's probably the worst I've seen since we opened."

"I'm emailing the owner this afternoon since I'm never able to catch him."

"Good." Judy stomps her way back through the front of the shop to clean up our outdoor area. We set up a few tables and chairs out front so customers can enjoy their treats beneath the cute white and yellow striped awnings I had installed as part of the renovations, but we have to bring them inside when we close. We learned our lesson the hard way. We made the mistake of leaving them outside on the first day we opened and we found them strewn all over the street the next morning.

A couple of our regular customers breeze in through the door as soon as I flip the *open* sign. Yep, we already have regular customers. *Pinch me now!*

"Morning, Carol. Morning, Wayne." I smile as I welcome them, then return to the counter, ready to make their usual coffee order. They're so sweet. They've been married for fifty-four years, and they still hold hands. They've been stopping by every morning since we first opened, so they get their coffee on the house now.

"Morning, Harry. We missed you yesterday. To celebrate having you back, today's the perfect day to enjoy one of your delicious breakfast croissants." Wayne smiles.

I chuckle. They always have a new excuse for enjoying something or other. "It sure is. Take a seat and I'll get started. Carol, same for you?"

"Yes, dear. That'd be lovely. Did you enjoy your day off?"

"I did. Thank you. Caught up with some things that I'd been neglecting at home." The café has been taking up all of my time, which was evident by the state of my apartment.

I grab two breakfast croissants and place them in the oven, then set about making their coffee. More people step inside, and I get caught up in the busyness of chatting with my customers and filling orders. Throughout the day, the three of us work together seamlessly, and before I know it, Judy's flipping the *open* sign to *closed* and we all take a collective breath.

"Holy almond croissant. Today was crazy busy," Judy says as she leans against the front door, her wide brown eyes glittering in the afternoon sunlight while she fixes her ponytail.

I nod, my smile wide and my feet and back aching. "Yep, but I wouldn't have it any other way. We sold every single croissant, and I could barely keep up with the crêpe orders."

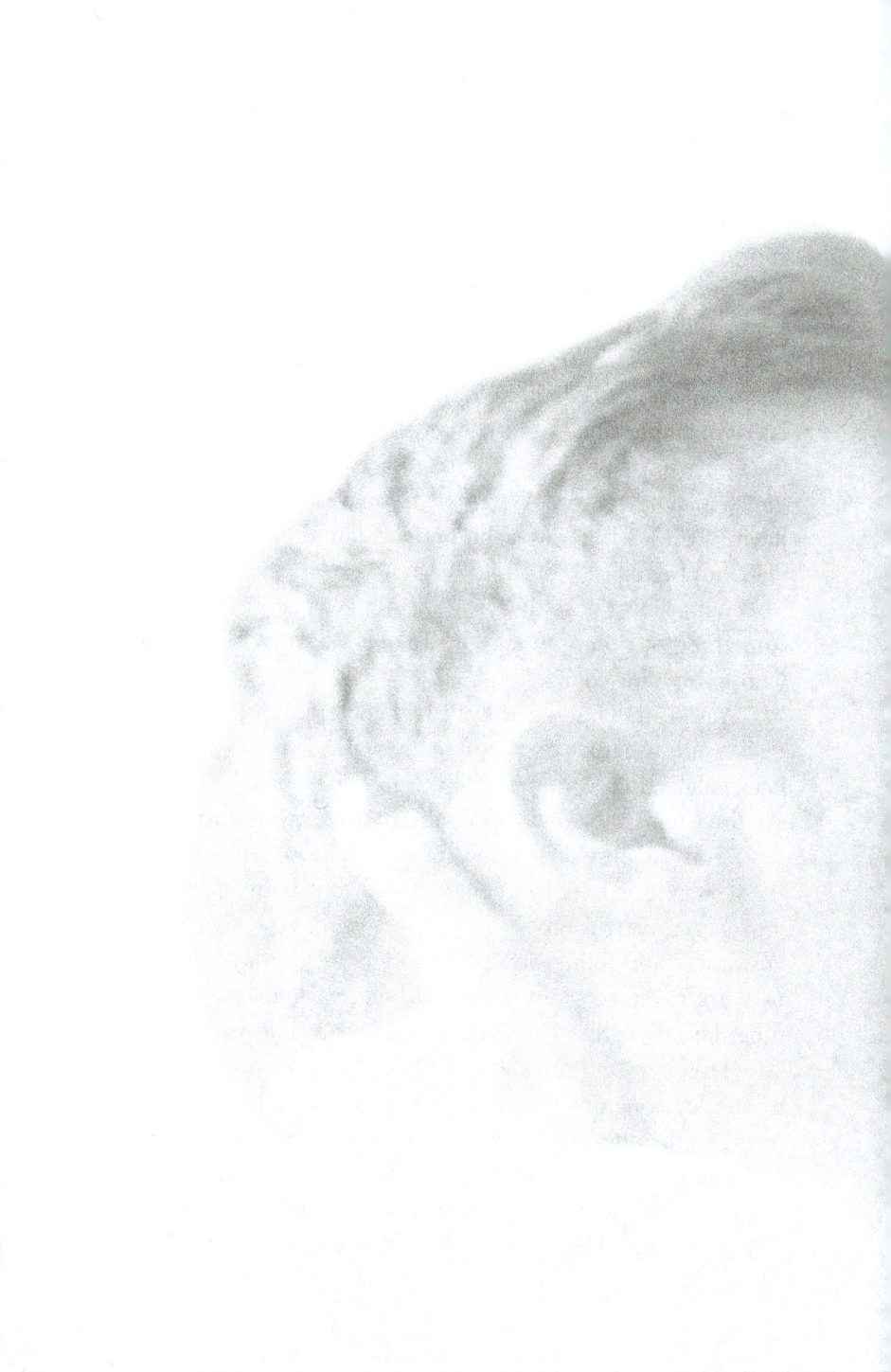

CHAPTER 2

—finn—

I FLOP INTO MY CHAIR IN MY QUIET OFFICE AFTER MIDNIGHT. It's been a day. One would think after the celebrations yesterday, today would have been quieter because people were nursing hangovers. *Nope.* Today was one of the busiest Tuesdays we've had in months.

This is the first chance I've had to check emails, and it's the last thing I feel like doing, but I need to keep on top of them or they get out of hand. I open my laptop and check the app.

Fifty-two!

Maybe I should hire someone to do this shit. Max has certainly been happier since he found himself an office manager. To be fair, that relationship turned into more than just a boss/employee situation. I smile, remembering the first time we all met Molly. The guys and I placed bets on whether or not they would hook up. Max has no idea we were betting on his love life, but it was fun just the same.

I make a start, working through solicitation emails, invoices, and responses from suppliers until I come across one with a subject line that catches my eye:

You need to take a good long look at yourself!

I glance down at myself and shrug, then read on.

From: Harry Dubois <harry@harryshouse.com>
To: Mr. Brady <manager@bradyspub.com>

Hmm, it came through late this afternoon. *Harry's House.* I scan my brain, trying to work out why that name is familiar. That's right. It's the new place next door.

Dear Mr. Brady,
I'm the new owner of the building next door, *Harry's House of Crêpes and Croissants*. On several occasions, I have stopped by to speak with you regarding issues that originate from your pub, only to find you unavailable or not on the premises. I am very busy and don't have time to keep chasing after you, hence this email.

Jesus, Harry sounds like he needs to get laid.

I would like to bring some urgent matters that require imme-diate action to your attention. Since opening my café one month ago, and even before that during renovations, my employees and I have had to deal with the aftereffects of your drunken and disorderly patrons running rampant down our street.
Almost every day, I arrive at work before dawn to be greeted with the sour stench of vomit and a vile mess on my back stoop.

Oh shit! That's disgusting. I retch at the thought of vomit. I'm a sympathetic vomiter, always have been, and it's not like I can completely avoid it here, but I do my best.

I've had to purchase kitty litter, industrial gloves, and additional cleaning supplies to deal with the mess. However, that is not the only mess we have to deal with. The stench of urine is another issue we must address daily. Your patrons seem to think it's acceptable to urinate at the front and back entrances of my shop and along the side wall which is facing the alleyway we share between our premises. As you can imagine, during our current summer, the smell is highly offensive, and the urine is unsanitary.

Well, shit.

Finally, each morning we must spend time we simply can't afford collecting trash left behind by your loitering patrons. Empty cigarette packets and beer bottles, used condoms, as well as napkins and cardboard coasters with your pub's name emblazoned across them—just to name a few items we regularly find surrounding our business.
By my calculations, I have spent $237.90 so far out of my budget cleaning the mess left behind by your patrons. Not to mention the numerous hours my staff and I have devoted to the cleanup, which should be spent preparing for our day.

Does he expect me to pay for the cleanup? There's no proof my patrons made the mess, and what the hell does he expect me to do about it, anyway?

Please see the attached photographic evidence.

I click on the images and scroll through a dozen photographs of vomit, trash, and what I'm assuming are urine stains on the stoop and along a wall, but really could be anything and not necessarily caused by patrons from my pub. I come to the last photograph, which clearly shows a pile of napkins and coasters. Well, shit. They're definitely from my pub. I click back to the message and continue reading.

I kindly ask that you take appropriate measures to monitor your patrons after they leave your establishment to ensure they do not linger in the area and cause such disruption to the surrounding businesses. If the issue does not improve, I'll be forced to take things further and contact our local council member.

What the hell does he expect me to do?

"Knock, knock." Callahan's voice breaks the silence in my office. He steps inside and places a glass of whiskey on my desk. "A nightcap." He takes the seat opposite my desk and studies me. "What's up?"

"We've pissed off the new neighbors." I tilt my head toward the new café next door and spin my laptop around so my night bar manager—and long-time friend—can read the email for himself.

He's quiet as he reads, and I take a sip of whiskey, enjoying the burn as I swallow. "Shit. He sounds like he's got a stick up his ass. What the hell are we supposed to do about our patrons once they leave here?"

"My thoughts exactly. Though, to be fair, they shouldn't be leaving here with bottles. I'm not exactly sure how that's happening, but it's easy enough to stop. I'll send a message to our team about ensuring patrons don't leave with bottles. The rest isn't our problem, and we can't be expected to do anything about it."

He nods and sits back in his chair, resting his ankle on his opposite knee. "Matthew stopped by again today. I sent him home with enough ingredients to make tacos for his family."

"Thanks. I meant to have it ready for him, but got caught

up filling in downstairs and lost track of time." I rub my chin, not sure how to broach an issue that's been bothering me.

Callahan lifts his chin. "What's up?"

Sitting forward in my chair, I lean my elbows on my desk. "Have you noticed anything strange about the stock?"

His brows furrow, and he takes a moment to think. "We seem to be going through more of the top-shelf stuff over the past couple of weeks."

I nod. "Exactly. But I haven't seen an increase in the reconciliation reports."

"Shit." He sits straighter. "Do you think someone's stealing product?"

"That's exactly what I'm thinking."

"I'll take a closer look at the books and inventory. Then I'll check the system for any reporting issues."

"Thanks. Keep it between us for now. I don't want to alert anyone that we're aware of what's going on until I know for sure."

"No problem."

We spend the next thirty minutes shooting the shit over whiskey. He leaves and I focus back on the email. I hit reply, then type.

Not my problem.

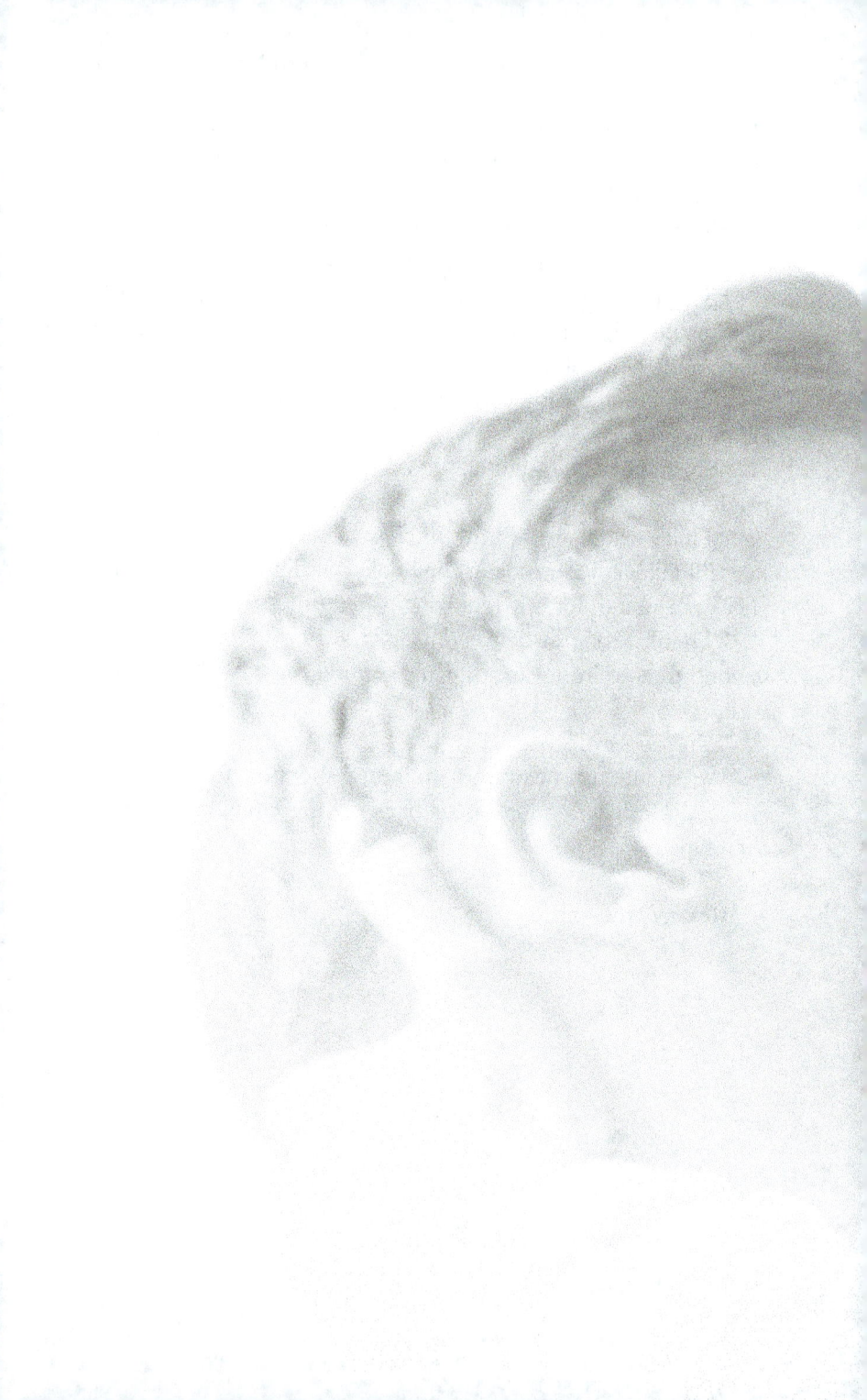

CHAPTER 3
—harriet—

I watch Quentin tuck Judy under his burly arm—her head barely coming up to his armpit—and leave, then slump heavily in my chair and open my laptop to check emails and place a supply order. I scan my inbox to check if the owner next door has responded to my email.

Yep, there it is.

A weight lifts off my shoulders knowing that he's going to take action, and we'll no longer have to deal with the mess. I click on the email to open it.

My eyes nearly pop out of my head, and I'm pretty sure steam is coming out of my ears. Three words. *Three simple words* which aren't normally offensive are waiting for me on the screen.

Not my problem.

With shaking hands, I push away from my desk and stand abruptly, sending my chair crashing into the wall behind me—to be fair, it's not like my office is huge, so it doesn't have far to travel. I lean back down and study my screen again in the hope that I read the email incorrectly. I scroll down the screen to see if maybe I missed something, but I haven't. What an arrogant jerk. I really shouldn't be surprised. Clearly, he doesn't give a shit about any of the businesses around him or we wouldn't be in this situation.

My blood boils. *What an ass.*

A knock at my back door steals my attention, and I glance at the time—that'll be my produce delivery. Sure enough, when I open the door, Stella's smiling. "Hey, Stella. How're things today?"

"Pretty great." She points over her shoulder. "I have your order."

"Awesome. Let's get it inside."

We work together to bring my organic produce order inside —placing it on my stainless steel counters—and chat as we work.

"I'm guessing things are going well since you had to increase your order."

"It's been amazing, Stella. More than I ever expected at this point."

"You've only been open, what … a month?"

"Yep. And we already have regular customers." I squeal on the inside. "It's honestly working out better than I hoped."

She rubs my arm. "I'm so happy for you. You deserve all the success, my friend." She heads out to her truck. "I'd better keep moving. I still have a couple of deliveries to make."

"Thanks, Stella. I'll see you tomorrow."

"Sure will."

I use organic locally grown produce wherever possible so I can do my bit to reduce my footprint, and it also helps my friend, Stella. I spend the next hour washing everything and storing it so it's ready to use tomorrow. Once that's done, I do a quick check of inventory before sending off an order for more essential ingredients, all the while ruminating on what my next step should be with my arrogant neighbor.

Another knock at the back door breaks through my musing. That must be Liam with my dairy and eggs. He recently took over for his father, who had to slow down when a cow kicked him in the thigh, breaking his femur. Because of the accident, doctors found he had bone cancer, and he's been having treatment to deal with it, leaving the responsibility of running the farm to Liam. I open the back door as Liam's heading back toward his truck to open the doors.

He glances over his shoulder with a handsome grin. "Hey, beautiful."

A blush heats my cheeks at his attention. He's asked me out a couple of times, but I can't bring myself to date a man eight years my junior. I know women do, and more power to them, but it's not for me. "Hey, Liam. How's your dad doing?"

He pauses and turns around to face me properly. Placing his hands on his hips, he drops his head to look at the ground, and my heart drops to my toes. "He had a fall last night." I grasp the collar of my shirt and step closer to him. "The chemo's left him frail, and he lost his balance. They did an X-ray to check he didn't break anything. It came back clear, thank God, but he's pretty banged up and bruised."

"Oh my gosh, I'm so sorry. If there's anything I can do, please just ask." I reach out and squeeze his arm.

"Thanks, Harry. Appreciate it."

"I have some croissants that didn't sell today. I'll package them up for your dad. I know how much he loves a Pain au Chocolat." I wink.

He smiles at me. "He'll love it."

Liam carries my order inside, refusing my help. While he loads everything into my fridge, I pack some leftover treats for him to take home and send him on his way.

I lock my bike to the fence, grab the package from my basket, and make my way toward reception. My heart aches with memories of visiting Grand-Mère Mae here. Dementia had taken its toll on her and she needed care I couldn't give her in the final year of her life. I hate that it came to this for her because she could no longer enjoy her favorite pastime— baking. I promised her I would continue to visit her friends, Frank and Beverley, as often as I could, so I set aside every Wednesday afternoon to do just that. I always sneak in a little treat for them, which puts a smile on their weathered faces. I sign in at reception and then head down the long corridor toward their rooms.

I knock on Beverley's door first, and she greets me with a warm smile and hug as soon as she opens the door. "Harry. It's so great to see you, my dear."

I squeeze her tight. "You too. How have you been?"

"Up to no good as usual." She snickers with a twinkle in her eye. When I grow old, I want to be Beverley.

I giggle. "I bet. You must keep the staff on their toes."

She winks at me. "I do my best."

"Shall we collect Frank?"

"Of course." I hold out my elbow, and Beverley loops her hand through. Then, we stroll a few doors down to Frank's room.

Beverley knocks, and when Frank opens his door, his eyes light up when they land on her. I've often wondered if maybe Frank has a crush on Beverley. "Hey, Frank. Look who's here to visit with us."

It's only then he spots me and his smile grows wider. "Harry."

I move in closer and give him a one-armed hug, holding up

the treats I brought with me. "I have treats. Shall we go to the visiting area, and I'll make you both a cup of tea to go with these?"

We wander slowly down the corridor at a pace Frank can manage with his walker. They get comfortable and I set about making them each a cup of tea, then join them in the club chairs. Frank never talks very much, but he joins in the conversation now and then, nodding along, and smiling at the funny things Beverley says.

After we've chatted about our respective weeks over tea and croissants, Beverley glances around and then whispers, "Let's play a game of poker." She tilts her hips and pulls out a bag of M&M's and a packet of cards from her pocket. "I brought my cards, and we can play for these." She wiggles the packet in front of us.

Frank chuckles. "Where'd you get those? We're not supposed to have them. Choking hazard. As if we don't know how to eat anymore. We may be old, but we still know how to eat," he grumbles.

She shrugs with a glimmer in her eye. "What can I say? My grandchildren love me."

"If we get caught with them, I'm blaming you," Frank tells her. I guess being in law enforcement for most of his life makes him a stickler for following the rules.

"Go ahead. What are they gonna do? Lock me up?" She holds out her hands with her wrists together toward Frank. "Go ahead, Officer Frank. Lock me up and have your way with me."

I spit out the tea I just drank, and I'm sure my eyes look like they're about to pop out of their sockets. Frank goes bright red, and Beverley taunts him by moving her hands up and down. "Oh my God, Beverley. You're too much sometimes." I chuckle as I wipe my mouth with the back of my hand. "I love you."

"Settle down, woman. There's a time and place for such things." Frank huffs.

"You're such a party pooper sometimes, Frank. I don't know why I bother. I'm quite the catch, you know."

Frank mumbles something under his breath, then says, "Are we playing poker or not?"

I grab the deck and shuffle. "Of course we are."

We spend the next hour playing poker until the dinner bell rings, signaling the end of my visit. We quickly stash the prohibited treats out of sight, and I say my goodbyes with tight hugs until next week. Climbing on my bike, I can't wipe the smile from my face. Since losing Grand-Mère, Beverley has kind of stepped into the role of being my grandmother, and I couldn't be more thankful.

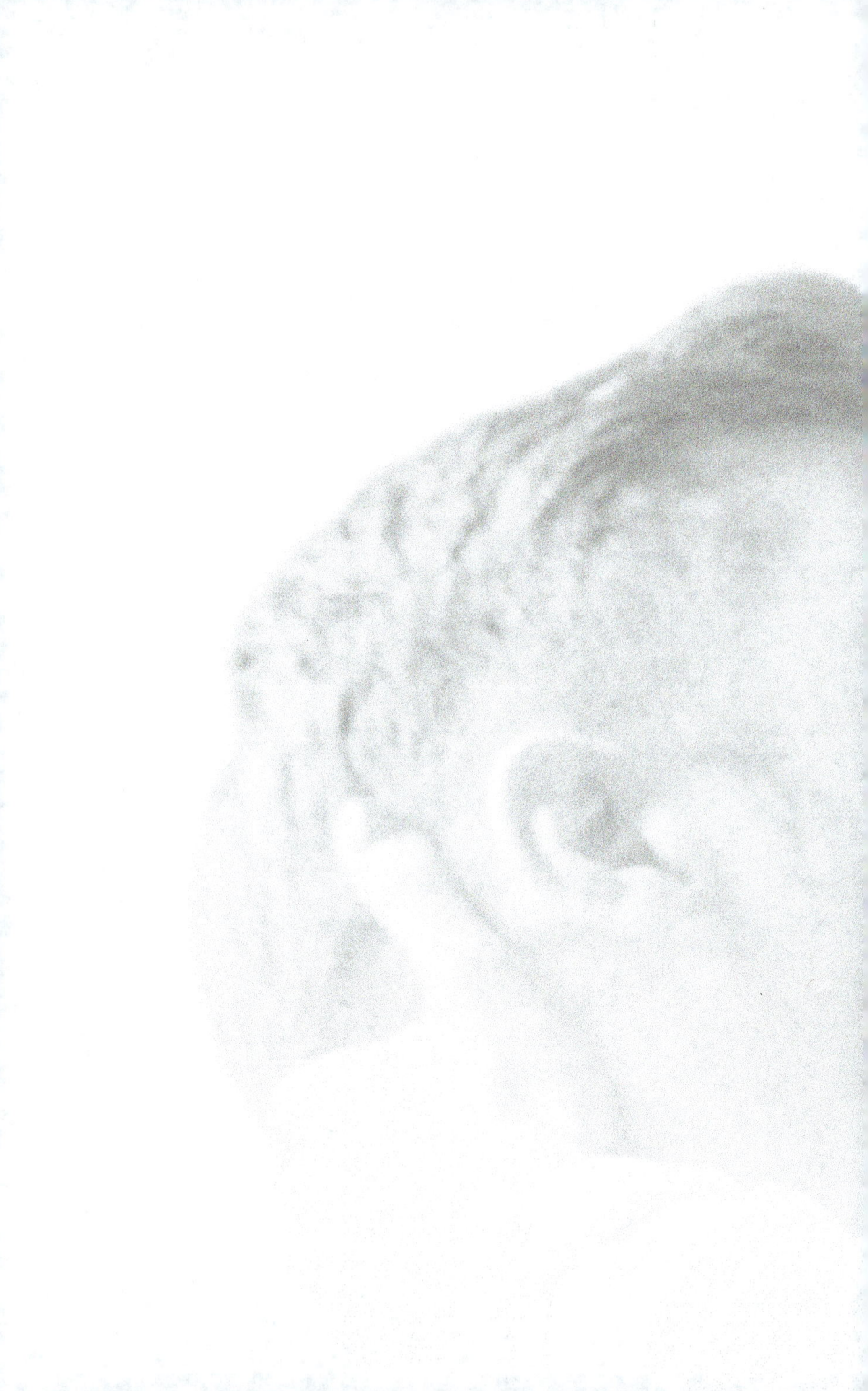

CHAPTER 4

—finn—

I PARK IN MY USUAL SPACE AND CLIMB OUT OF MY CAR. Glancing at the back area of the café across the alleyway we share with *Harry's House*, I notice everything appears to be clean; what the hell is Harry complaining about? I shove my hands in my pockets and head over to check out the side wall of his building and sure enough, I can see the stains shown in the photos. The closer I get, the more I notice the faint smell of urine. I crinkle up my nose and spin on my heel to head back to my side of the alleyway. Thank God people don't piss against my building.

As the back entrance to my pub becomes visible, so does a pile of trash, and I come to an abrupt stop. Placing my hands on my hips, I study the mess, noting the coasters, napkins, and is that a … used condom? I swivel my head back toward my neighbor and narrow my eyes.

What the fuck?

The sound of a truck pulling into the parking lot tears my attention away from the mess. Blaze climbs out of his black 4x4—which has flames painted along the sides—and is at my side in four long strides. "What the fuck is that?" He points to the pile of trash.

"A pile of trash," I reply dryly.

"I can fucking see that. Why is it at our door?"

I thumb over my shoulder. "I have a feeling our new neighbor was pissed at my response to his email."

Blaze narrows his eyes. "What email?"

"I'll show you when we get inside."

I grab a nearby crate and use it to scrape the mess out of our way, then unlock the door and disarm the alarm. Being my day head manager, I had already planned to tell him about the email to keep him abreast of the situation. He follows me into my office, and I fire up the laptop to show him the email. "Have you seen Harry? He says he's been over a few times to speak with me about it." I point to the screen, highlighting the sentence.

Blaze shakes his head. "Nope. Some chick that works there has come in a couple of times asking for you. But not Harry. You want me to go over and have a chat with him?"

I wave off his offer because he's an intimidating guy—if he's not working, he's at the gym—and I don't want to misstep with our new neighbor any more than I already have. "Nah. I'll let it go this time. If it happens again, I'll head over there and deal with it." I spin the laptop back around and pull up our staffing schedule. We spend the next thirty minutes working through the schedule for the next two weeks and then separate to prep for opening.

"Morning, boss."

"Hey, Miss Sylvia. How's Mick?"

"He's better today. Sorry I had to leave early yesterday."

"No problem. Family first. Always."

"Thanks, Finn." She points over her shoulder. "I'll get the chili started."

I smile at my cook. She's been working here since I was a

kid. I'd occasionally come and sit in Dad's office during school vacations, and she'd have me "taste test" her cooking, but it was really an excuse to feed me because that's what she does; she feeds people and takes great pride and satisfaction in her work. "Thanks, Miss Sylvia." She told me to drop the Miss, but I can't—it feels disrespectful.

I head to the storeroom to check the inventory, noting the items with low quantities, then wander back to my office to place an order. The time before the pub opens is always busy with the amount of prep that needs to be done. There isn't a minute to waste.

For the past five mornings, I've arrived at work to find a heap of trash piled at our back entrance, and today is no different. It's like Groundhog Day. I get that Harry somehow thinks I have control over what my patrons do after hours, but this has gotten out of hand. Blaze has a short fuse and is probably angrier than I am about what's been happening. I'm worried he's going to go off the deep end, so I quickly clear the mess before he arrives. I'll find time to visit Harry today; this has to stop. I glance across at the rear of the café, just as I have each day, hoping to catch someone so I don't have to go inside. I don't want to make a scene in front of customers if I can help it.

A group of our Tuesday regulars—who come in to enjoy lunch and a couple of beverages after their morning bowling competition—wave as they head out. "See ya next week, guys," I call from where I'm wiping the bar. Checking the time, I glance around and figure now's as good a time as any to head next door. I'm not sure when they close, but it must be almost time. "I'm heading out for a bit. Won't be long," I tell Macy.

She's the best cocktail bartender I have. Women, in particular, come from far and wide for her concoctions, while men come far and wide to watch her because she's beautiful.

"No problem. I think I can manage the two suits in the corner." She smirks.

I raise my brows. "I bet you could."

She throws her head back and a raspy laugh escapes her. The two suits look our way, and even *I* notice the look of appreciation in their eyes. Stepping out into the bright afternoon sunlight, the heat almost sears my nose hairs. Fuck, it's hot out here. I forget how hot it gets outside during the day. By the time I leave work in the early hours of the morning, the city is considerably cooler.

When I arrive next door, I stop short when I spot customers entering the café. A petite woman wiping the outdoor tables notices me. "We're closing in ten, so if you want something, you'd better head inside."

I glance through the windows regarding the line and decide to come back in thirty. "Thanks." I raise my chin toward the counter where a beefy guy—who I'm guessing is Harry—is serving the customers while a woman with chocolate-colored shoulder-length curly hair and a gorgeous smile makes coffee. "I need to chat with Harry, so I'll come back."

Her friendly expression turns into a frown. "Sure."

I wander up the street to the market and buy an apple. I rarely keep fruit at home because I spend barely any time there. Sometimes I wonder why I have a place when I spend so much of my time at the pub, but I need somewhere to sleep, I guess. I peruse the other market stalls and find a new stall that specializes in candles. Mom goes crazy for candles, so I stop and smell a few, hoping to find one I think she'll like. They all smell a little chemical-y to me, so I pass. Mom won't like them.

Checking the time, I think I've given Harry enough time to close, so I wander back toward the café. As luck would have it, he's out front, packing up the tables and chairs. Approaching the guy, I hold my hand out. "Hi. I'm Finn Brady, the owner of *Brady's Pub*." I hitch my thumb over my shoulder toward my building.

He immediately scowls at me. Standing straight, he ignores my outstretched hand and crosses his beefy, tattooed arms across his chest. I'm not sure what I was expecting a café owner to look like, but this wasn't it. He looks like he should run people through a military-style gym routine, not sell pastries. "You're the asshole from next door." He takes a menacing step toward me, and I take a step back. I can hold my own if I need to against someone around my size but I'd have no chance against someone like Harry.

The woman from earlier steps outside. "You're back." I nod and before I can say anything, she continues. "Harry's inside."

Huh? I thought I was speaking with Harry.

I look back at Mr. Muscles. "You're not Harry?"

He shakes his head. "Nope."

Right. I breathe a sigh of relief. "I'll head inside, then." Let's hope Harry's a little less intimidating.

Opening the door, I step inside to find the woman I saw making coffee earlier and make my way toward the counter. When she notices me, her smile is instant, and it looks even more spectacular up close like this. "I'm sorry we're closed, but if there's something in the cabinet you'd like, I can easily wrap it to go for you."

"Sorry. Not a customer. I'm here to speak with Harry. Is he around?"

She tilts her head to the side, and her bright gaze, which reminds me of springtime grass, studies me closely. "And may I ask who you are?"

I realize how rude I've been, so I hold out my hand. She slides hers into mine, and I swear a tingle of electricity shoots through my fingers and makes its way up my arm. I snap my eyes back to hers to see if she felt it too, but there's no sign she felt anything. "I'm Finn Brady. The owner of the—"

She snatches her hand from mine and narrows her eyes at me. Those sparks I was feeling in my hand are now shooting from her eyes. "Pub next door," she snaps. "The man who thinks that what happens down our street and to the surrounding businesses isn't *his* problem." Her words are laced with venom as she folds her arms across her chest, drawing my eyes down to her moderate-sized breasts—anything more than a handful or mouthful is a waste anyway. A smirk touches my lips. "You think that's funny?"

I snap my gaze back to her face. "Huh? What's funny?"

"You just smirked at me, you arrogant ass." She huffs. "You think it's funny that your patrons run amok and create havoc for the neighboring businesses?"

"No. Of course not. Look, I came to speak with Harry about it. Would you mind telling him I'm here to see if we can come to some kind of agreement?"

Snickers sound from the front door, and I glance over my shoulder to find the man and woman from a few moments ago watching us.

"*I'm* Harry," the woman behind the counter snaps, drawing my attention back to her.

"What?" That can't be right. "*You're* Harry?"

"Yep. Do you have a problem with that?" she taunts.

I drop my gaze back to her tits, then slowly make my way to her gorgeous face, noting the freckles scattered across her nose and cheeks. "Not at all."

Well, life just got interesting.

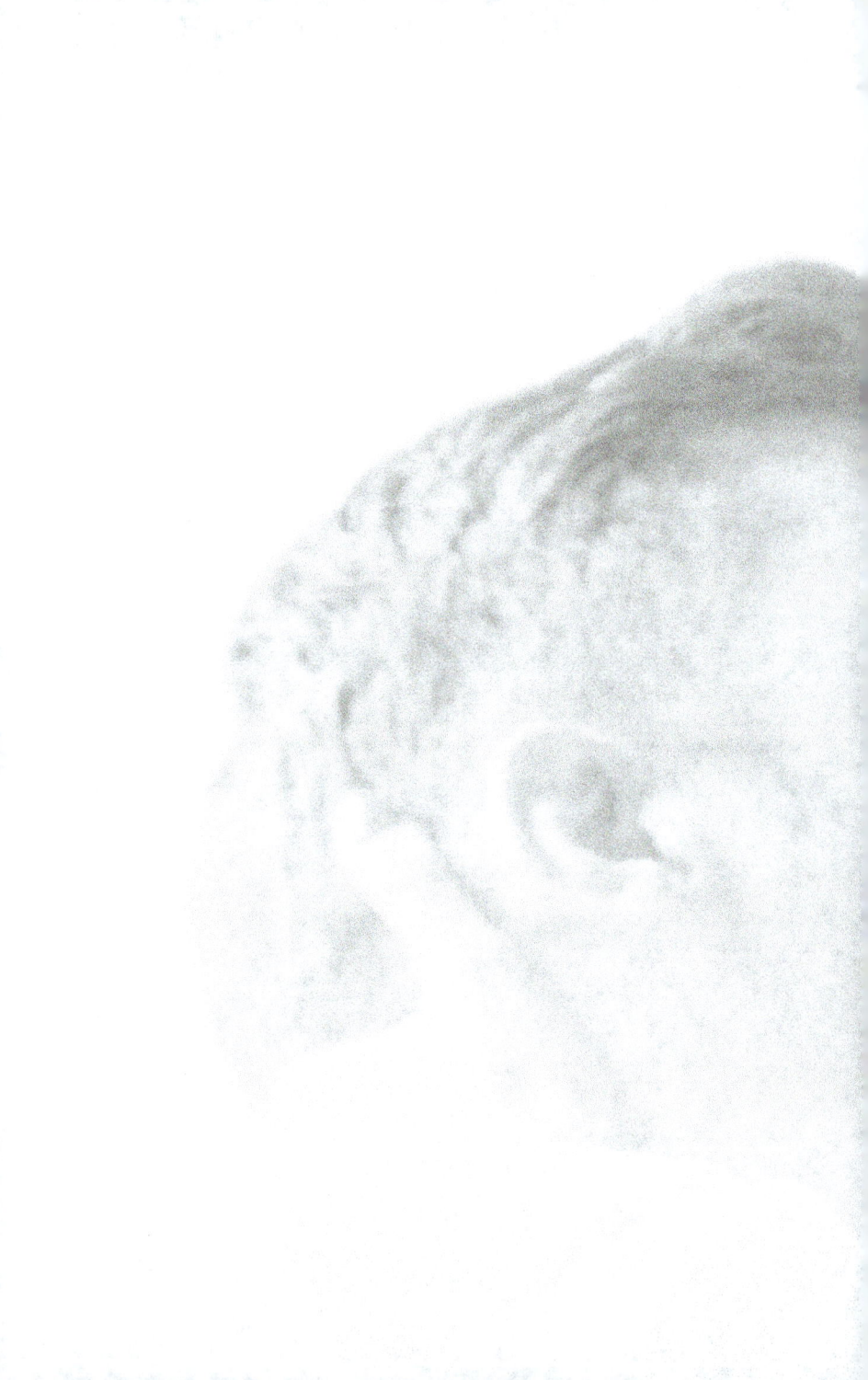

CHAPTER 5

—harriet—

The nerve of this asshole. A hot asshole——with his tousled hair that's the color of wheat, a perfect amount of scruff on his stupidly handsome face, and broad shoulders tapering down to a trim waist——but an asshole just the same. *Ugh!* I shouldn't be noticing any of that because the man standing in front of me is an arrogant, self-centered jerk.

I'm glad I'm wearing my full apron today or he'd be able to see my nipples trying to break through my bra under his perusal. *Damn it!*

I'm not sure what I was expecting my business neighbor to look like, but it certainly wasn't this. In my mind, I imagined an older, balding man with a pronounced beer belly and breath that smells like my father's. I know I'm being unfair and making an assumption, but that's where my mind automatically goes.

"Have you finished checking out my boobs?" I snap.

Tilting his head to the side, he rubs his temple with his finger, a smirk touching his lips. "I'm not sure I'll ever be finished checking out your boobs, to be honest."

Oh shit! I can't believe he just said that. Heat races through my body, spreading to my neck and cheeks.

I catch Quentin moving toward us, his fists bunched at his sides and the veins in his neck protruding, so I hold up my hand to let him know I can deal with this asshole before he goes all protective big brother. "Would you guys mind cleaning the kitchen while I speak with Mr. Brady?"

Judy grabs her husband's hand and drags him through to the kitchen. "Sure thing." It's a comical sight, and if I wasn't so pissed at the man standing in front of me, I'd have to laugh. There's no way Judy could move the mountain that is her husband if he didn't *want* to move.

Once I'm alone with the asshole, I turn my attention back to him. "Your response to my email was downright rude and unprofessional."

He places his hands on the counter and leans forward with narrowed eyes the color of the sky. "I don't know what you think I should do. I can't be expected to follow my patrons home," he fires back.

I lean forward over my side of the counter. "Maybe you could make sure they're not so intoxicated when they leave your premises that they have no idea what they're doing or how they're behaving," I snap. Surely he has some obligation to his customers to ensure their safety.

"I can't watch every single person who comes into my pub. We have a no-service policy for anyone we think is getting close to the limit. But as I already said, I can't follow them out of the pub to ensure they behave. Maybe you should look at the area outside of your café and ask yourself why you're being target-ed." *I know he didn't just blame me for the never-ending mess left by his patrons.* A red haze forms around the edge of my vision. He stands upright, folding his arms across his chest with a smug grin, like he's solved all of my problems. "I've had no complaints from any of the other businesses around me. In fact, I've never had any complaints." He raises a single, golden brow.

I mirror his stance, and his eyes drop back to my boobs, so I drop my hands to my hips instead. "Well, I'm complaining, and I'll keep complaining until you do something about it. I'm sick of coming to work every day to wade through trash and the mess left behind by *your* patrons."

"You have zero evidence that *my* patrons are causing the mess." He points to his chest.

I narrow my eyes at him. *He didn't.* "I sent you photos clearly showing your bar coasters and napkins. You can't stand here and tell me it's not your patrons making the mess. And what about the beer bottles? There isn't another pub close by."

He softens a little. "Well, yeah, maybe they drop a napkin or coaster here or there, but you can't prove the other stuff is from my pub. Do you have video evidence?"

"Here or there? Are you for real right now? And no, I don't have video evidence, but I do have photos clearly showing items with your pub's name plainly printed." I huff. My head's spinning. Does he really think he can deny the evidence?

"Well, yeah."

"You realize that, as a business owner, you have responsibilities to the community. It's your civic duty." His mouth draws tight, almost like he's trying to hold back a smile. "That's okay. I'll contact the council and see what they say about it all." I raise my nose in the air in defiance. *Ha!*

He holds his hand out in front of him as if to stop me. "Now, now. There's no need to involve the council. I'm sure you wouldn't want them to know about the pile of trash you're leaving at my back door each day, now, would you?"

What in the actual fuck? I narrow my eyes. "You have no proof I'm leaving anything at your door, so don't even go there."

His lips spread wide. "Well ... actually, I do." He's so freaking smug.

I narrow my eyes and my heart races. *What if he does have proof?* He could get me into a lot of trouble. "Bullshit."

He raises his brows and his eyes hold a glint that says, *I got you!* "Not at all." He digs into his back pocket, drags out his phone, and presses the screen a few times, then turns it around so I can see. I recognize the location. It's the back area of the pub. "I, unlike you, have security around my property." *Oh shit!* "So when I look back over my saved footage, I clearly see you dumping trash at my back door."

I see red. "Well, if your patrons weren't such pigs, I wouldn't have to collect the damn trash, and if you had responded to my email like a civic-minded person, I wouldn't have had to stoop to such low tactics to get you motivated to do something about the problem." My voice rises with every sentence until I'm almost shouting.

"Calm down," he says as he holds his hands up as though he's warding off an attack. I can't believe he thinks telling a riled-up woman to calm down is okay. Maybe this guy is more of an idiot than an asshole.

I grit my teeth. "You did not just tell me to calm down. I have every right to be angry. You've done nothing to help the situation, and you stand there like your shit doesn't stink and tell *me* to calm down. Get out!" I fling my arm out toward the door, but he doesn't move. "I said, get out. Get out of my café and never come back here."

That stupidly sexy smirk appears again. "You're fucking stunning when you're angry. Anyone ever tell you that?"

That's it. I step around the counter, my lungs heaving with my anger, and press my hands against the hard planes of his chest to push him out of my café. "I've asked you to leave. Now get out." I push and he moves a little, but I'm pretty sure it's only because he wants to.

"If you wanted to touch me, all you had to do was say so. I wouldn't mind."

"Aaaah!" I almost scream as I continue to push him toward the door. Geez, he smells good. Damn him. He finally moves. "Get out before I grab one of my rolling pins and hit you over the head with it."

He chuckles—*chuckles*—and holds his hands up in surrender. "Okay, okay. I'll leave, but we still need to work out this issue."

I open the door and he stops on the threshold so I can't close it. "You stop your patrons from being pigs. Simple. Problem solved." I give him a false saccharine smile. "Goodbye." I shove him hard and he breaches the doorway enough that I can slam the door closed. I flick the lock and give him a smug smile.

He blows me a kiss and salutes me, his eyes sparkling in the afternoon sunlight. Why did he have to be so damn good-looking? "Later, Little Firecracker," he calls through the glass.

Ugh! I turn my back to the door and stomp my way through to the kitchen. Once I'm out of sight, I lean back slightly to peer around the door frame to make sure he's gone. Yeah, I'm definitely only watching to make sure he leaves. He's standing with his hands in his pockets and a grin I want to slap off—

"What are we looking at?" Judy's voice startles me, and I jump out of my skin as she moves into the doorway, in full view of the windows where Finn is standing.

I grab her hand and yank her back. "Shh. You scared the bejeezus outta me."

She chuckles and tries to peer around me. "He's hot."

Quentin clears his throat. "Did you forget I'm here?"

"No, love. Just making sure Harry noticed how hot her neighbor is."

I roll my eyes and huff out a breath. I noticed. I'm not blind.

"So long as that's the only reason you're using the word 'hot' to describe another man while I'm in earshot."

Judy moves closer to Quentin. "I only have eyes for you. You know that." She bats her lashes at her husband and presses onto her toes to land a kiss on his chin. He softens and gives her the smile he saves for her as he brushes her sun-kissed bangs out of her eyes.

"Okay. You guys should head home. I can finish up here."

I get them out the door and then slump against it, blowing out a long breath. When I bring my hands up to rub down my face, they're shaking from my confrontation with Finn. I drop my head back against the hard surface, looking up at the ceiling.

I can't possibly be attracted to the asshole next door.

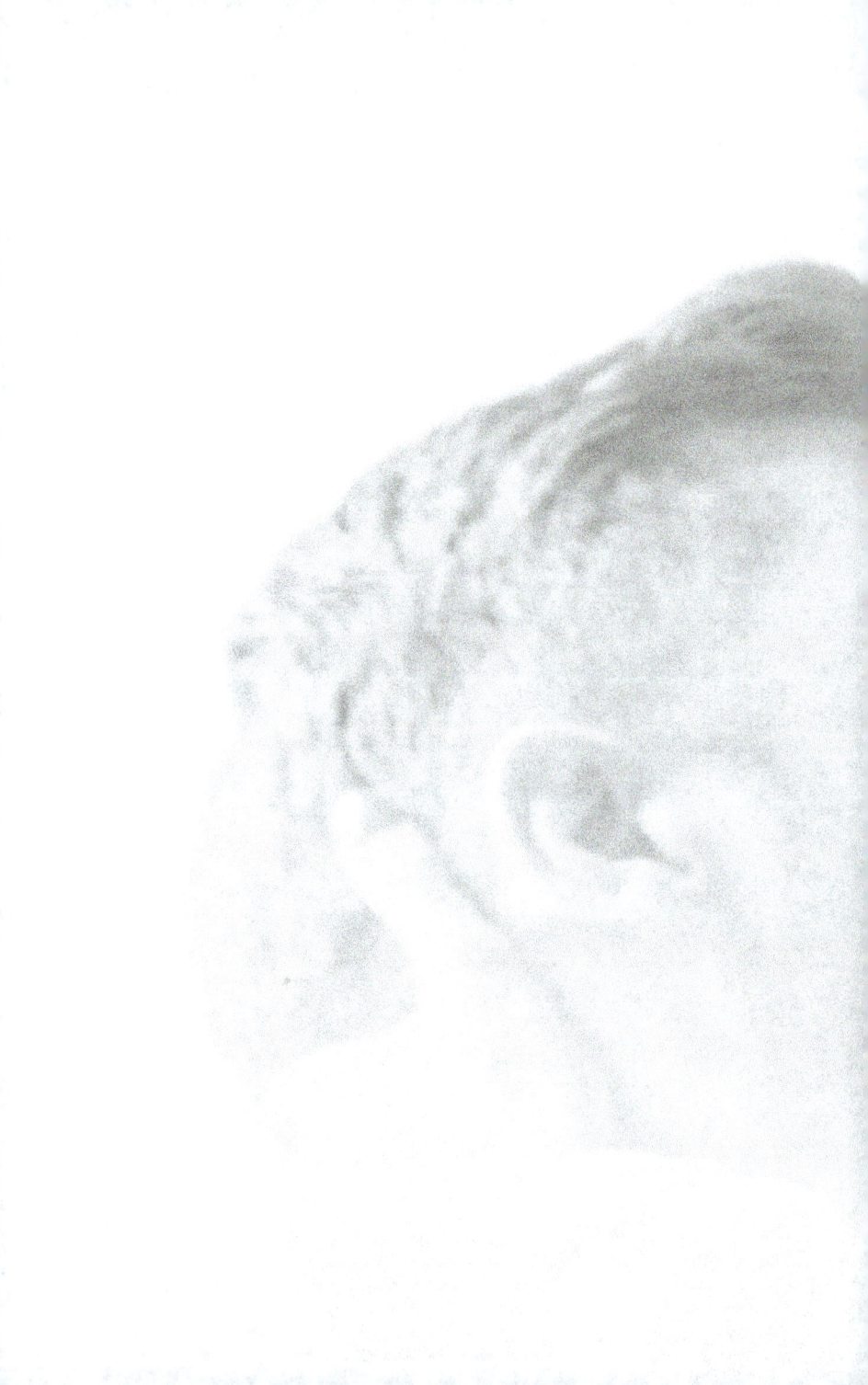

CHAPTER 6

—finn—

I SET THE ALARM AND STEP THROUGH THE BACK DOOR. THE security lights flood the back area, and as I lock the door, I glance across to Harry's place with a smile that instantly drops when I notice how dark it is around her building. No wonder people are loitering there when they leave my pub. It's the perfect place to take a piss or have a quick fuck.

I glance at my car and then take off toward the café. Using the flashlight on my phone, I look around and sure enough, there's shit from my pub scattered all around. Sighing, I head back, unlock the door, disarm the alarm, and gather the supplies I'll need to clean up the mess, as well as a couple of flashlights to light up the area.

My phone buzzes in my pocket and when I pull it out to answer, the name of my security company lights up the screen. "Hello."

"Mr. Brady. This is Nix from *Steele Security*. We noticed unusual activity regarding the alarm at your business premises. We wanted to check everything was okay."

I rub my temple. "Yeah, Nix. Everything's fine. Just had to

step back inside to collect some stuff. I'll reset the alarm in a few."

"Sure thing. So long as everything's okay."

"It is."

"Good. I'll leave you to your night."

I quickly rush before he disconnects the call. "Hey, Nix?"

"Yes, Mr. Brady."

"Do you have time to stop by tomorrow late afternoon or early evening? I need to speak with you about something I want to have done."

"Sure. Would five suit you?"

"Perfect. See you then."

I start by picking up the trash, noting there are no bottles. Good to know the staff got my message loud and clear about ensuring no bottles left the premises, but there are plenty of napkins and coasters ... and a couple of used condoms. Disgusting. I move closer to the building, collecting trash, when I step into something squishy. When I shine my light at my feet, I groan.

Fuck!

Retching, I step out of the mess and screw up my nose as I move as far away as I can. I look around for a hose but come up empty, so I head back across to my place and drag my long-ass hose behind me to wash the area. Fucking dirty pigs. Can't hold their damn liquor. No wonder Harry's so pissed. I wouldn't like to arrive at work to this every morning either.

I freeze when I realize she said she starts before dawn. It would be as dark as it is now when she arrives. What the hell is she thinking? Anything could happen to her. Anyone could wait in the dark for her. To do anything to her. It just takes one nut job to take a liking to her and watch her routine to know when they could do the most harm.

My anger at Harry's lack of personal safety fuels me as I clean up along the side and out front of her café. As soon as

I'm finished, I dump the trash in my dumpster, lock the pub, and reset the alarm.

Pulling into my driveway, my headlights shine on my small home. I stop and study it—the dark windows, the lack of plants, the empty porch—and I know when I walk inside, it will feel as empty as it looks from the outside. I've resigned myself to this empty life. Who would want to be in a relationship with someone who's barely around? The pub takes up most of my time, leaving very little for anything or anyone else. Monday night soccer games with my friends are the only time I get for myself. I'm not sure how Mom and Dad's marriage survived all the years he spent running the pub; maybe that's why I'm an only child.

Leaving my shoes on my porch so I can deal with them in the morning, I head inside, grab a glass of water, and make my way to the shower. I need the warm spray on my tired muscles. I'm proud to be the second generation to own the pub, but the long days are fucking exhausting. As I turn on the faucet and wait for the water to heat, I think back to my childhood and how I rarely spent time with my father. I would have to beg him to take me to work just so I could be with him, and even then, his days were busy and our time together wasn't what I would consider quality time.

I turn my body, letting the hot spray rain down over my shoulders, and my thoughts turn to earlier when I discovered Harry isn't a man but is instead a sexy little firecracker. My lips tip up as I recall the sparks flying from her eyes as she schooled me on my civic duty as a business owner. A low chuckle bubbles up and escapes.

Fuck, she's hot.

When she told me to get out of her café, I wanted to tug her into me and steal her anger with a kiss that would make her forget what she was so pissed about. My cock swells, and I glance down at it. "Not tonight, buddy." My hand won't be as satisfying as seeing Harry's angry lips wrapped around the base of my dick while I choke the fury right out of her.

Climbing out of the shower, my cock taps against my stomach as if to remind me he's there. As if I could forget; I'm pretty sure my balls are blue. Rubbing my body dry, I can't ignore the ache any longer. Widening my stance, I drop my towel, swipe my palm with my tongue, and wrap one hand around my rigid length as I gently tug my balls. I just need to take the edge off or I won't be able to sleep.

Closing my eyes, I tighten my grip and drag my hand from the base to the tip, rolling my palm over the crown to collect the precum that's leaking from the opening. I imagine Harry's tongue lashing across the head and my dick jolts in my hand. As I rub my cock with rough strokes, I imagine Harry on her knees looking up at me with fire in her eyes as she licks my dick and my breaths falter. Picturing my cock disappearing between her angry lips has my hips pistoning forward as I pillage her mouth; her eyes watering as she struggles to swallow my cock. The image is enough to send electricity shooting down my spine, and I know my orgasm is imminent. Increasing my strokes, my vision grays around the edges as I point my dick toward the sink and let loose.

Ribbons of cum decorate the porcelain and I groan at the thought of painting Harry's lips with it. I slow my strokes, catch my breath, then clean up my mess and climb into bed, feeling mildly sated but unsatisfied.

I'm closing out the tab for a group of businessmen who've been here since one when Nix walks through the door. He spots me behind the bar and makes his way toward me.

"Mr. Brady." Always so damn formal.

I hold out my hand across the bar. "Nix. How many times have I told you? Call me Finn."

"Sure. Sorry. It's a throwback to my upbringing and my days in the military."

"No problem. Would you like a drink?"

"Maybe after we've finished discussing business. You're my last stop for the day, then I'm on my own time."

I nod. "Sure thing. Follow me." I step from behind the bar, leaving Blaze to manage on his own, and Nix follows me outside. I can't see any movement next door, which is exactly what I wanted and why I made the appointment for later in the day. "I'd like to set up some motion sensor lights on that building." I point to Harry's café. "Particularly at the front and back entrances, along the side, and the lot out the back. Apparently, my customers like to linger there and leave a mess behind, and I think it's because it's so dark."

"Yeah, that would make it an attractive place to linger." He steps toward the building, and I follow him as he makes his inspection. "Any security?"

"Not sure. It's not my building. I just want to deter people from hanging around after leaving my pub."

He nods. "Sure. I think two lights out front, one on the back door, then two lighting up the back area, and two along the side should do the trick."

"Sounds good. How much to supply and install?"

He rubs his chin. "Probably looking at two grand."

I raise my eyebrows in surprise and whistle. "Shit."

"Yeah, they're not cheap, but in terms of low-end security, they're a great idea and effective."

I nod and rub my temple. "Fair enough. I get that. When would you be able to install them?"

"Let me check my calendar. I have the lights in stock, so it's a matter of finding a time." He digs his phone out of his back pocket. He frowns at the screen, shakes his head, then brings up his calendar. "I have next Thursday morning available or late Friday afternoon."

"You'd need access to the inside of the building to wire them in, right?"

"Yep."

"Okay, late Friday afternoon then. That way it won't impact her business."

"I'll book it in. I'll need half upfront to secure the job."

"Send me an invoice, and I'll sort it out." We head back toward my bar. "The owner can't know I organized the lights. I'll need you to contact her and tell her a local philanthropist is helping small businesses with their security measures as part of a community safety project, and let her know when you'll do the installation. Or something along those lines."

Nix raises one eyebrow. "You're asking me to lie?"

"Well, sort of. *I'm* being philanthropic." I shrug as I open the door to the pub and nod for Nix to enter. "She's pissed at me about my customers making a mess around her café and demanded I do something about it."

His eyes narrow. "So, tell her you're doing something about it. She'll be happy."

I step behind the bar, ready to make Nix's drink. "What'll you have?"

"I'll have whiskey, thanks." He moves to get his wallet out, but I wave him off.

"On the house." I pour him a generous serve and slide the glass across the timber surface. "I don't want her to know I'm trying to fix the problem. I like having her pissed at me."

Nix barks out a laugh. "You're fucking weird, man."

I shrug. "Maybe."

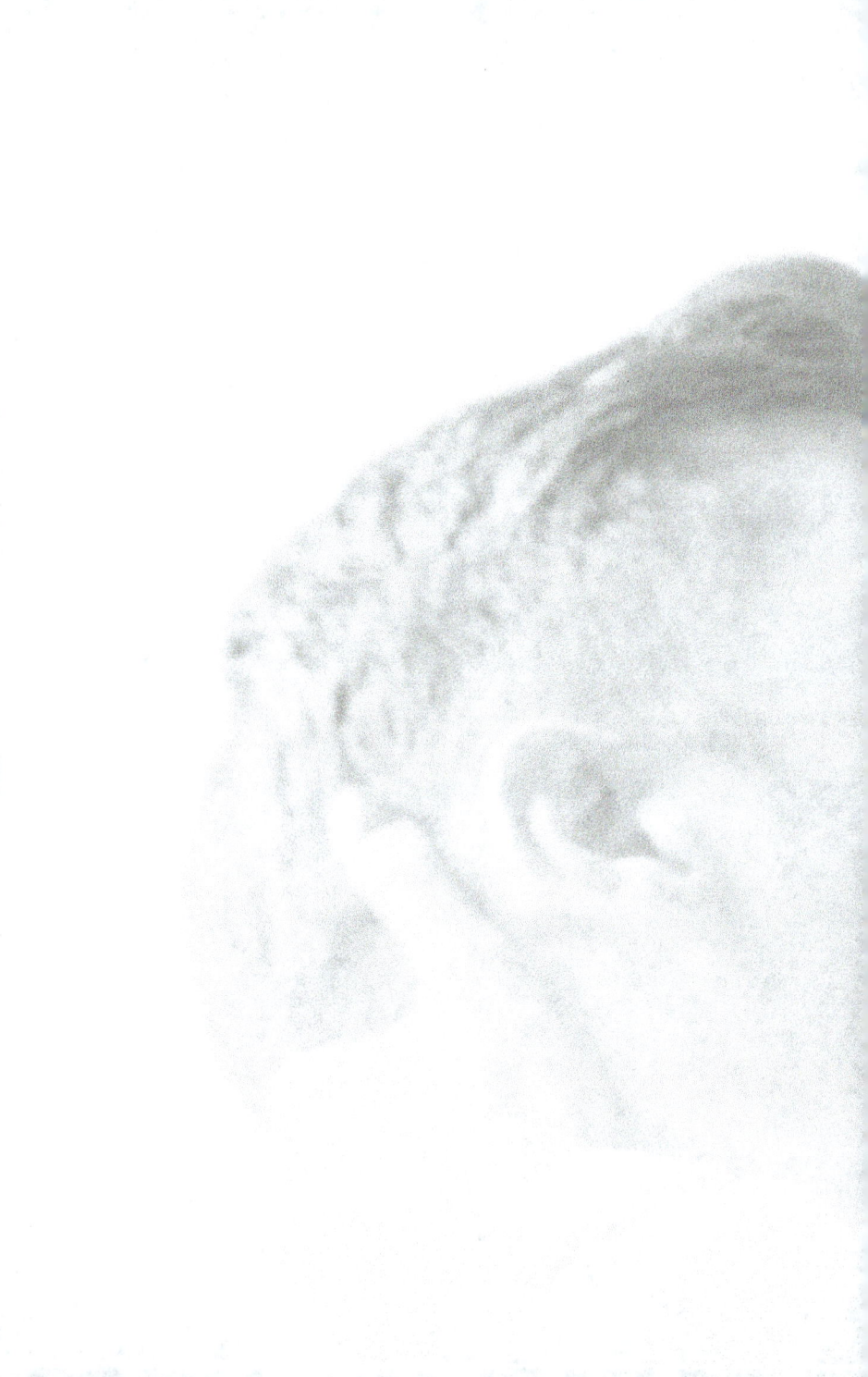

CHAPTER 7

—harriet—

"Harry, phone for you," Judy calls as I finish serving our last customer for the day.

I smile and wave goodbye as they exit, then lock the door and flip the sign to *closed*. When Judy hands the phone to me, I check the screen but don't recognize the number. "Hello."

"Hello. Is this the owner of *Harry's House of Crêpes and Croissants*?" the rich, masculine voice asks.

"Yes, it is."

"My name is Nix Steele, and I'm the owner of *Steele Security*. I've been engaged to install motion sensor lights at various small businesses within the city to improve security and community safety. Your business was selected to have security lights installed. I have you on my calendar for tomorrow at five p.m. for the installation. Will that suit you?"

"Uh." My mind's gone blank. I had no idea something like this was available. I suppose it might help to make my premises less appealing for unsavory activities in the middle of the night. Although since my *chat* with Finn, things have improved. I haven't had to clean up a single thing, which has been a welcome change and I'm no longer running behind with my morning routine. "That would be great. What do you need from me?"

"I'll need access inside your premises to wire the lights properly, which will probably take an hour or two. It'll mean I need to turn off the power to your café."

I nod, then realize Nix can't see me. "And it's completely free?"

He pauses for a moment. "Yes, ma'am."

"Okay. I'll be here and you can have all the access you need. Thank you, Mr. Steele." I hadn't considered security lighting, but it makes sense.

"You're welcome. See you on Friday." Well, this is a pleasant bonus. It'll be great for when I arrive in the morning, too.

Quentin and Judy have already cleaned up out front, so I work on closing down the kitchen.

"What was that about?" Quentin asks.

I explain what Nix said and when he's coming to install the new lights. All the while, Quentin's eyes narrow as he rubs his chin—it's his thinking action. "That sounds suspect. I can't imagine anyone spending that sort of money without wanting something in return. I would follow up and maybe double-check with the council."

My mood deflates. "Really? Why would someone want to do something like that?"

He shrugs. "I dunno. There are weirdos around. Give the council a call."

Once they've gone, I make myself a coffee and decide to follow Quentin's advice.

"Good afternoon, City Council Offices, Emily speaking."

"Uh, hi, Emily. I'm not sure whom I need to speak with, but I wanted to talk to someone about a program installing security lights to improve safety for small businesses."

"Oh. I'm not familiar with that program. Can you please hold?"

"Su—" Elevator music fills the line before I even agree. I check my emails and find a confirmation email from *Steele Security* for the installation of seven motion sensor lights. I do a Google search for the company and it comes up at the top of the results. Clicking on the link, I locate their community review rating. Four point eight stars. That's pretty good.

"Hello, are you still there?"

"Yes."

"Sorry for the delay. I've spoken with everyone I can think of who may know something about the program, but nobody's heard anything about it. I'm sorry I couldn't help you."

Hmmm. "But I have a confirmation email here from *Steele Security* to install the lights tomorrow afternoon. Do you think it's legitimate?"

"I'm sorry. I can't help you."

I thank Emily and disconnect the call, even though I have more doubts now than when I first called. The guy seemed genuine on the phone, and the email and website look professional. I wonder who's behind the initiative? I read the information on the *about* page and learn Nix is former military. He's a handsome older guy in that stern kind of way that I assume comes from being in the military. I study the photo of him closely to commit him to memory.

Right at five o'clock, the squeak of brakes near my back door alerts me to Nix's arrival so I make my way outside. I don't want to be trapped inside in case the guy is unsavory. At least outside, I can shout for help or run away. Bold letters clearly show STEELE SECURITY on the van along with company details, including their business license number. I snap a quick photo. Everything seems legitimate. When the driver climbs out, he's definitely the guy from the photo on the website except with a few more grays at his temples, which make him look distinguished. I blow out a relieved breath because I don't think I have anything to worry about.

It took some convincing to get Quentin to finally leave this afternoon. Once I told him the council knew nothing about the security light initiative, he wanted to stay back with me to make sure I was safe. If it weren't for Judy reminding him about his nephew's basketball game and that there are plenty of people close by at the pub, I think he would still be here.

Nix approaches me with a warm smile that transforms his face from harsh to friendly. "Hello. You must be Harry."

His hand slides into mine. "Yes. You must be Nix."

"Yes, ma'am. Would you like me to show you where I plan to install the lights?"

"Sure. But I have one quick question."

"Shoot."

"Who's behind this initiative?"

He shifts on his feet but doesn't break eye contact. "A local philanthropist who would like to remain anonymous."

"Oh. Okay. So I won't be able to thank this … philanthropist?"

"I can pass on your gratitude."

Hmm. "Okay. Thank you. I'll shoot you an email and perhaps you can forward it on my behalf."

"No problem." He walks around my premises and I follow behind as he shows me where he plans to install each light. "I'll get to work. I won't need to come inside for a while. When I'm ready, I'll knock on the back door.

I smile at him. "Sure thing. Can I get you a coffee, shake, or anything before you start?"

"Thanks. I'm okay."

I leave him to do his work and head inside. Cleaning my cupboards will help me pass the time for the next few hours. Stacking the equipment onto the workbench, I almost have everything out except the stuff at the back. The cupboard is so damn deep I'm going to have to practically climb inside to reach it. I push the items at the back toward the front of the cupboard, then wiggle backward. Climbing to my feet, I place the items on top of the workbench and spin around.

"Aaaah!" I bring my hand up to my chest to prevent my heart—which is now pounding furiously—from escaping. "Oh my God, you scared the crap outta me! What the hell are you doing here?"

His eyes burn a path from my hips, pausing on my breasts, and one side of his mouth lifts as his eyes finally make their way to my face, which I'm certain is as red as a tomato. "Enjoying the show."

I narrow my eyes and shove my hands on my hips. "I'm pretty sure I told you to get out and never come back."

He raises an empty container, shaking it from side to side. "I ran out of sugar and don't have time to make a trip to the store. I didn't think you'd mind giving me some, and I'll replace it tomorrow."

"I'm usually gone by now. What would you have done then?" I snap. His eyes drop to my mouth and I swallow the urge to lick my lips. God, just being in this man's presence fires me up in more ways than one. He must have some wicked powerful pheromones pumping out of his pores.

He takes a step closer to me and tilts his head to the side. "Well, I would have to make a store run. But I know you're all about being civic-minded, so I'm sure you wouldn't mind helping a neighbor."

I take a step closer and stand tall, bringing the top of my head to the bottom of his scruff-covered chin. I hold my breath so I don't draw in any more of his seductive scent. "I'm not feeling very civic-minded today. Run along."

He brings his free hand up to his chest. "You wound me, Harry."

"Not my problem." His lips spread, and it's sexy as hell. I need to get this guy out of here before I do something I'll regret. "You can wipe that smug smirk off your stupidly sexy lips," I snap.

"Make me," he challenges.

My eyes narrow and my breathing becomes labored. This close, I can see the flecks of denim in his light blue eyes, which are currently being swallowed by his dilating pupils.

He edges closer and we're almost standing toe to toe. It wouldn't take much to close the distance. He tips his lips up again and I see red. I press up on my toes and close the distance in a moment of insanity, fueled by frustration and … intense desire. My lips touch his and I swear to God and all that's Holy that sparks fire through my body. Within the next moment, his hand is wrapped around my waist, pulling me flush to his muscular body, and I can't miss the bulge pressing into my stomach. His tongue slides across my lips, making them tingle, and I open with a gasp as he slides his other hand into my curls, tugging my head to where he wants it, and slips his tongue inside to tangle with mine. It's a vicious kiss, full of fight and frenzy, and weeks upon weeks of frustration. I grip the loops of his jeans, holding him to me as we each fight for dominance.

"Okay, I—" A rich, masculine voice breaks through my lust haze and I push away from Finn until my ass hits the counter behind me. Trying to catch my breath, I touch my fingers to my swollen lips as I scan my kitchen to work out whom the voice belongs to. Nix stands at the back door with wide eyes flicking between me and Finn. "Sorry to interrupt, but I've installed the lights outside. I need to work inside now to connect the wiring. I'll need to turn your power off."

"Sure." I wave my shaky hand around my kitchen, which is currently in disarray, much like my thoughts. "Do whatever you need, and I'll try to keep out of your way."

Nix steps further inside and places his tools on the floor, then steps back outside.

I spin around to face Finn. Now that I've had a moment to compose myself and catch my breath, embarrassment floods me.

I kissed him.

How stupid can I be to kiss this asshole? A sexy asshole who most definitely knows how to kiss, but an asshole just the same. I wave my finger at him. "Never do that again." Even though that kiss was completely my fault.

"Aww, don't be like that, Little Firecracker."

"Don't call me that either." I flick my arm out, pointing toward the door. "Now get out."

"That's not very neighborly of you." He picks up the container and shakes it, seemingly unfazed by our kiss. He probably goes around kissing everyone like that. My mood spirals to a dark place thinking of Finn kissing other women. "How about some sugar?" He winks at me. *Cocky much.*

I growl. Literally, growl. My anger doesn't seem to faze him. In fact, it seems to spur him on. I draw in a deep breath and paste on a fake saccharine smile. "Sure." I hold out my hand for the container, then make my way into my pantry, ensuring I keep the smile plastered to my lips. Dragging out the heavy tub of sugar, I pop the lid and fill his damn container, screw on the lid, seal my tub of sugar, and slide it away. I turn to leave and bump into a hard body, stopping me short. "Damn it."

Finn brings his hands up to my hips to prevent me from

losing my balance and once again, our lips are within kissing distance.

Do *not* kiss him. Don't even look at his lips.

My eyes drop to his lips without permission, and the asshole drags his tongue across the bottom pillow seductively. He steps forward and I step back. He does it again, and when I step back, I'm trapped against the storage shelf—the hard metal digging into my spine. The heat from his body seeps through his clothes and mine, scorching me as he raises one hand to rest against the shelf above my head. He looms over me and I need to tip my head back to maintain eye contact. The small space is charged with anticipation; the air thick with lust and tingles erupt through my body. I'm working hard to fill my lungs with oxygen, but it's a struggle as I try to block out his scent. He leans closer and his warm breath ghosts across my lips. Tilting his head to the side, he presses his lips to mine, gently at first, as if he's testing the water.

I *should* push him away. I *should* tell him to stop.

I shouldn't be opening my mouth and sliding my tongue across his lips, inviting him to deepen the kiss. His hand tightens on my hip almost to the point of pain, and he delves into my mouth, giving and taking, pillaging and building a desire so strong I'm ready to climb him like a tree. I fear my heart is trying to break out of my chest with how hard it's beating

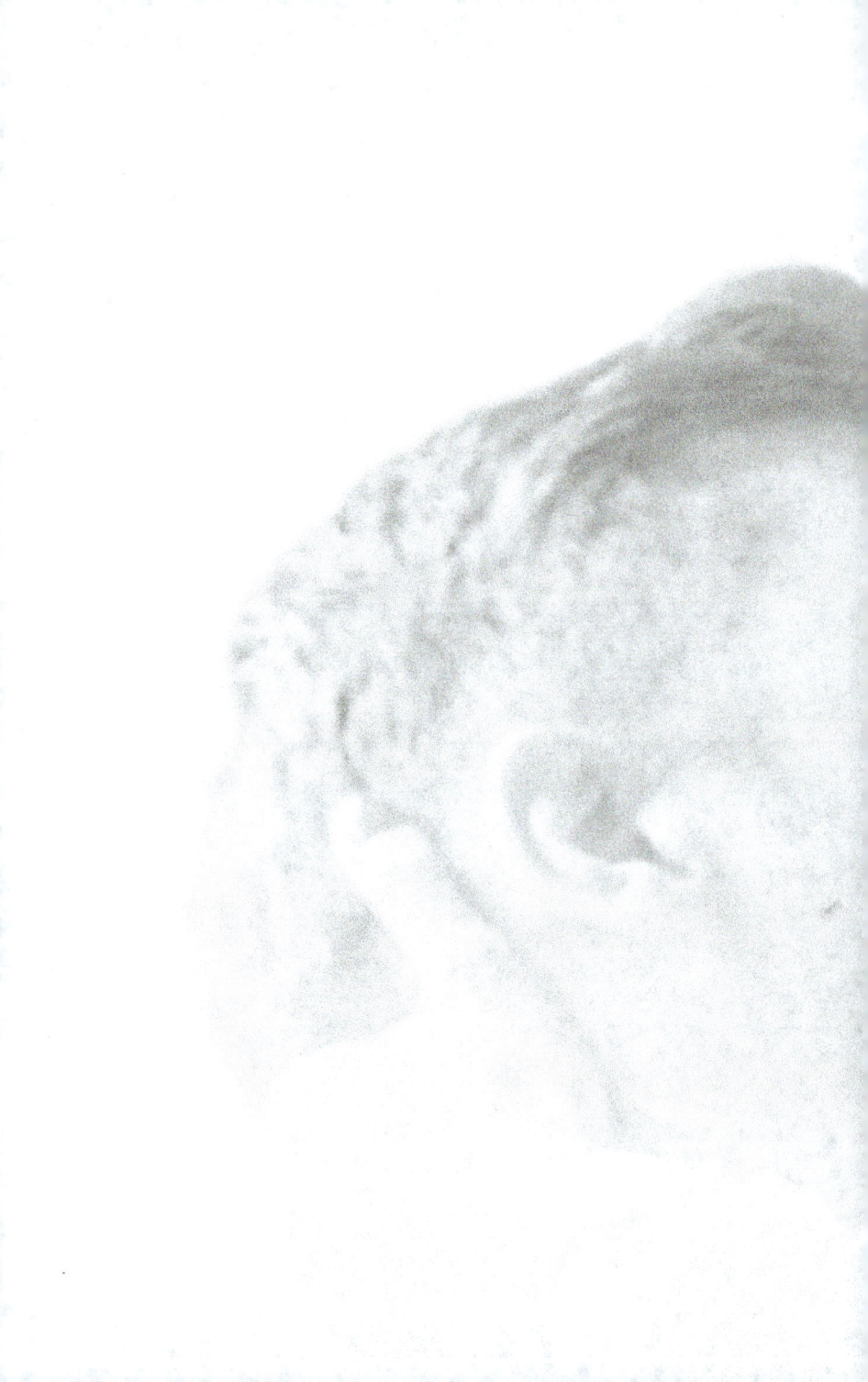

CHAPTER 8

—finn—

I KNEW THAT FIRE INSIDE HER WOULD TASTE INCREDIBLE. I JUST had no idea *how* incredible or how instantly addictive I'd find her. The desire to consume her becomes my sole reason for living, and I press into her to deepen the kiss, swallowing her soft moans. Dragging my hand up from her hip, I trace the dip of her waist until I come to her pert breast and cup it.

Harry rips her mouth from mine and, with a look of confusion, pushes me away. The action is so sudden; it catches me off guard and I stumble slightly. It could also be because all the blood is currently filling my cock, and I'm light-headed. Her wide eyes flick around the pantry as if she's trying to work out where she is. One side of my mouth tips up with satisfaction that my kiss has her so discombobulated. "I'm gonna need to do that again, Firecracker."

Her eyes land on me and narrow as she pushes away from the shelf I had her pressed against. "Don't do that again." She shoves my container filled with sugar into my chest—hard. "Take your damn sugar and get out." Her arm flies out to the side, and she points toward the exit. "Go."

With my heart hammering, sending my heated blood

racing through my veins, and my head spinning, I step back and hold the container of sugar over my head. "I'll be back, Firecracker." I spin on my heel to leave before she shoots me with those sparks lighting her eyes. So fucking beautiful.

As I pass Nix's van, he steps from behind it. "So, uh, Ms. Dubois wanted me to pass on her appreciation to the philanthropist paying for the lights." He waves his hand around. "But I'm assuming she's ... uh ... already thanked you?"

I glance around to ensure Harry's not close by. "Nah. She wasn't thanking me for anything, and she doesn't know this was me, and I'd like to keep it that way."

Nix nods. "Sure. Anyway, she's grateful for the lights."

"Great. Remember to send me the invoice."

I head back to the bar, knowing I'm going to make it my mission to have my lips on Harry's as much as humanly possible.

I push the door open with my foot. "Hey, Matthew."

"Finn." He steps forward to take the box of food from my arms. "Thanks for this. I really appreciate that you feed us every day. It's the only decent meal we get."

Matthew was rummaging through my trash cans for food when I first met him. I dragged him out by the scruff of his shirt and demanded he tell me why he needed to scrounge for food. I almost cried like a baby when he told me about his mom and family at home. We struck up a deal, and he's been coming by ever since. He's a good kid trying to do the right thing for his family.

"No problem. How's your mom doing?"

"She's really sick and she can't keep any food down." He glances down at the pavement between us and when his eyes find mine again, they're glassy. "The chemo's kicking her ass."

My heart sinks and I reach forward to squeeze his shoulder. "I wish you'd take the money I've offered."

He shakes his head. "Nah, man. I can't take your money. I feel bad enough about taking food from you every day. You *could* give me that job I've been asking for. That would help us out."

I tuck my hands in my pockets and drop my head. "You know I can't do that, Matthew. I'm sorry. Our employment policy is twenty-one. It's too risky otherwise. Once you're twenty-one, I'll happily give you a job, man."

"That's three years away. I can't wait that long. I won't leave the kitchen. Chain me to the sink if you have to. I promise I won't drink any alcohol." His eyes are full of honesty. "I've been asking around for work, but no one will hire me." He shrugs and I look at his clothes, then at his unkempt hair. This kid needs a break and if I can help him somehow, then that's what I'll do.

"I'm sorry, man. If I could, I would. People can be judgmental assholes. What if I gave you some money for some clothes and a haircut or something? It might help."

"You already help us so much." He raises the box of food to make his point.

"Giving you food only helps you in the short term. We need to get you employed."

He swallows. "I know. I'll think about it. Okay?"

"Okay."

Dad pulls into the alleyway, parks behind my car, and climbs out of his Volkswagen Golf with a face like thunder. Matthew turns back toward me. "Anyway, I'd better get home. Thanks again, Finn."

"No problem. Enjoy and say hi to your family for me."

Matthew heads off, disappearing around the corner as Dad

approaches. He's waving a sheet of paper above his head, and looking pissed. "What the hell is this?"

"Hi, Dad. How are you?"

"Don't *hi dad* me." His Irish brogue is thick when he's pissed, even though he hasn't lived in Ireland since he was a young lad. "Why in the hell are we paying to install motion sensor lights on the building next door?" He waves his arm out toward Harry's café.

I wince at the volume of his voice. Luckily Harry isn't outside to hear his outburst. "If you stop shouting and come inside, I'll explain."

We wander inside, Dad huffing and puffing behind me, ensuring he makes his displeasure known. I stop at the bar, pour us both a glass of whiskey, and then head into the office that used to be his but is now mine. I sit behind my desk to remind him I'm now running the show here, not him. He was the one who insisted he was ready to retire and wanted me to take over, but in times like these, I think he forgets he's no longer in charge.

He drops into the seat opposite my desk, takes a sip of his drink, and then sits back. "Well?"

I explain what's been happening, show him the email and the photos, and tell him how I started cleaning up the mess every night before leaving. "I'm exhausted by that time. I just want to go home and sleep, not spend an hour cleaning up shit our patrons leave over there."

"That's bullshit. What our customers do once they leave here is not our responsibility. You had no business spending two thousand dollars on lights for a building that isn't ours. What happens if we need to do some repairs or maintenance here?" he blusters.

"We have enough of a cushion, Dad." He huffs. "And if it comes to that, I'll pay it back out of my wages. I don't care. I was doing the right thing. The civic thing for a business that shouldn't have to deal with shit left behind by our customers."

"Next thing I know, you'll be supplying lights down the street because our customers use the damn sidewalk."

I roll my eyes. "Now you're being dramatic, Dad." I take a sip of my whiskey and change the subject. "How's Mom?"

His eyes sparkle. It amazes me that after forty-five years of marriage—a tough marriage because Dad had to dedicate a lot of time to the pub—that my parents are still in love as if they were newlyweds. "Mom and I have decided to visit family in Ireland. We're in the early planning stages."

My lips widen. "That's great, Dad. You guys deserve to treat yourselves to a vacation. You've worked hard and Mom sacrificed a lot."

He nods solemnly. I know he appreciates her quiet support. If it weren't for her running the home and raising me without complaint, *Brady's* wouldn't be the pub it is today.

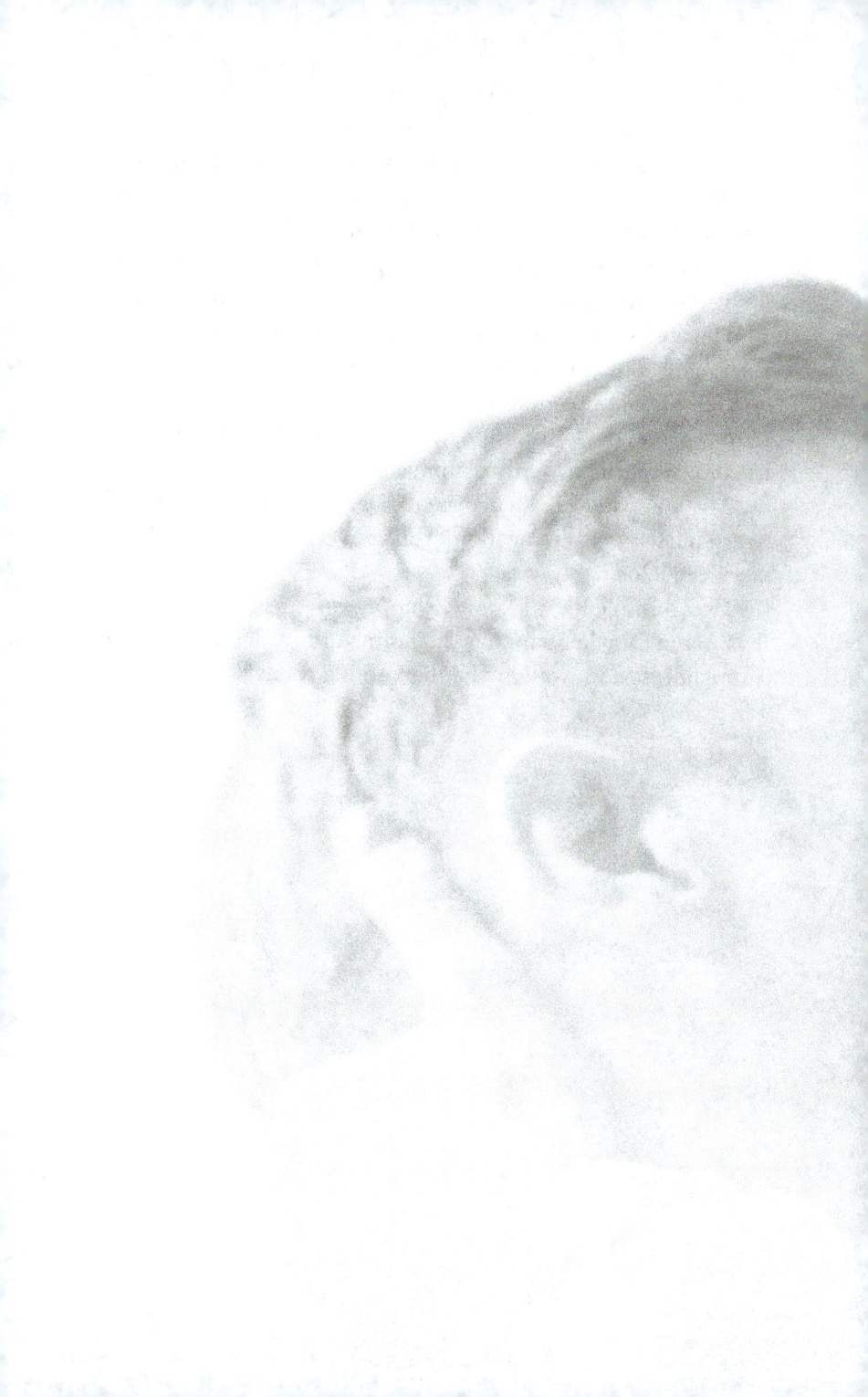

CHAPTER 9

—harriet—

I HAVEN'T SEEN OR HEARD FROM FINN SINCE OUR HEATED kisses, and I think it's for the best. I don't need another asshole in my life. At some point, I should take heed of the red flags and stay away—but he was such a great kisser and his body felt incredible pressed against mine. My cheeks heat at the memory and my sex tingles at the thought of him kissing me in other places.

A cup slides across the counter, breaking into my thoughts. "Excuse me, sorry to be a bother, but I ordered a weak latte. This one's a little strong."

I smile at the woman. "I'm sorry. I'll make you a fresh cup. It's not a bother at all."

"Thank you so much. I swear you could just wave the coffee over the top and it'll be perfect." She chuckles and I join her.

"Not a problem. If you'd like to take a seat, I'll bring it over." She returns to her seat, and I make her a fresh cup now that Quentin's returned to the kitchen. He can be a little heavy-handed with the coffee beans sometimes. He doesn't understand why people order weak coffee, and even though I love a short black, I get that people have different tastes.

Stepping out from behind the counter, I take the lady her coffee, and as I spin around to make my way back to the counter for my next order, a familiar face wearing a familiar smirk swaggers through the door like he belongs here. I curse my heart for picking up speed and my legs for turning to rubber. How dare he step foot in here. And while I'm with customers, to boot. I can't very well tell him to get lost. It would be unprofessional.

I glare at him, then spin on my heel and strut confidently—as if my legs are made of steel, not rubber—back to the counter, only to hear him chuckle behind me. Straightening my spine, I serve the next two customers efficiently and then curse myself that I didn't take longer, so I could delay the inevitable interaction I have to have with *him*.

He steps forward. "You're looking as gorgeous as ever today, Firecracker." His blue eyes twinkle with mischief. He knows I have to be civil to him in front of my customers.

Ignoring his compliment, I give him a tight smile. "Welcome to *Harry's House*. What can I get for you today?" There, that sounded professional.

He chuckles under his breath, then leans forward to rest his hands on the counter, his eyes skimming my mouth. "Another kiss would be great," he whispers, so only I can hear him.

I narrow my eyes. "Not happening. If you're not ordering, I suggest you step aside so I can serve my customers," I grit between clenched teeth. I'd love another kiss, but that would be stupid.

His lips tilt higher on one side and his eyes sparkle—the various shades of blue dancing with silent humor. "Keep that shit up, Firecracker. It makes me hard." He adjusts his pants, and I want to scream at him to get out. When I glance behind him, I remind myself I need to remain professional.

"Are you placing an order, Sir?" His eyes widen and I instantly realize my mistake. *Damn it.*

"Sir. I like that." He leans across the counter, bringing him closer to me. "You can call me that next time we're in private … if you like." He leans back and winks, then peers up at the menu board. "What would you recommend?"

My brain spins, and I take a moment to realize he's switched gears. "Any of the croissants are great for takeout."

"Oh no. I want to sit and enjoy my meal here."

Damn him. Of course he does because he gets off on torturing me. I paste on a fake sweet smile. "Would you prefer a croissant or a crêpe?"

"Crêpe, I think."

"Sweet or savory?"

"Savory. With a bit of fire. I love some spice and heat." I roll my eyes and his smirk returns.

I'll give him spice and heat. "Certainly." I smile tightly. "I have the chili crêpe, which you may enjoy. Will that be all?"

"Sounds great. I'll have a short black as well, please." He reaches into his back pocket and pulls out his phone to pay when I ring up his order. He taps the counter before stepping away to find a table, and I breathe a sigh of relief that he's no longer in my vicinity. I'm definitely not admiring his ass as he strolls away. I serve the customers who were in line behind him, noting it's almost closing time.

Judy takes over the counter so I can make the crêpes, adding extra chili to Finn's order for good measure. I should feel bad, but as much as I dig deep to find the emotion, I can't. Does he still deserve my ire since the issue that was initially a problem seems to be resolved? Probably not. But I need to hold on to my annoyance with him to maintain the necessary distance. Besides, he's shown no remorse for his response to my email. Plus, he owns a pub. And as a pub owner, I bet he drinks all the time. I swore I'd never date a man who drinks on the regular.

Drawing in a deep breath, I take Finn's crêpe to his table, along with his coffee. I place his food on the table, when, in reality, I'd dearly love to tip the plate upside down in his lap—I grin at the thought.

"Service with a smile. I may have to come here more often." Maybe I *should* have delivered his food to his lap after all.

My smile drops and I narrow my eyes. Leaning down to keep my conversation private, I whisper, "That's because I spat in your food." Not that I did, of course. That would be unhygienic and completely unethical.

A loud rumble of laughter bursts out of him and he turns so he can whisper in my ear. "We've already exchanged spit, or did you forget?" His warm breath ghosts across my ear and a shiver races down my spine. *How could I forget?* It's been on constant replay since it happened.

"Eat your food and get out," I snap. Standing to my full height, I smooth down my apron and spin on my heel, dismissing him. I busy myself behind the counter, covertly watching him take his first bite of the chili crêpe. His eyes widen and his mouth drops open. I snicker to myself but then notice his face is turning an alarming shade of red.

Shit! Maybe I took it too far.

He glances around and when his eyes land on the self-serve water station, he rushes toward it, pouring himself a glass of water and then gulping it down. He repeats the process, and I start to feel bad. Finn carries a bottle of water and his glass back to his table and retakes his seat, coughing quietly into his elbow. Once he has himself under control, he glances toward the counter and our eyes lock. His lips tip up on one side as they usually do and he salutes me. I tip my head toward him and serve my next customer with a gut full of guilt.

Should I go next door to apologize? I feel terrible that I acted out of anger and caused Finn so much distress. It was completely inappropriate, but worse than that … it was out of character for me. A knock at the back door interrupts my prep for tomorrow, as well as my thoughts. I pull it open. "Hey, Stella. How's …" My words and my smile die when I lay eyes on the man who always seems to be at the forefront of my thoughts.

He stalks forward and I have no choice but to back up inside. Once he's clear of the doorway, he closes the door behind him with an expression I can't read. "Not Stella." His stalking continues until I'm pinned against the stainless steel work counter in the middle of the kitchen; the cold steel digs into the lower part of my spine.

The air is thick with tension, and I swallow past the boulder-sized lump that's formed in my throat as Finn leans over me, pressing his fists to the steel on either side of my hips—our faces mere inches apart. His warm breath feathers across my lips. "Did it feel good, Firecracker?" I open my mouth to apologize, but Finn shakes his head and presses his thumb over my lips. He traces my face with his eyes and my tongue pokes between my lips to taste his digit when I definitely shouldn't. "Whatever comes out of your mouth next better not be an apology."

It's ironic really. Finn brings out a side of me I'd long forgotten, but he seems to like it, and I don't know how to reconcile that. It's a side I've spent my life burying deep because my parents did everything they could to squash my fire. They didn't like it when I questioned them or when I pushed back against their endless list of rules and expectations. I think it's the reason they dumped me with Grand-Mère instead of taking me with them on their travels. I lock my gaze with his. "Why would I need to apologize? It's not my problem you can't take the heat." I tip up my lips, waiting to see what his response will be.

Instead of responding with words, he surges forward and takes my mouth with his. Our teeth clash and our tongues duel. He pushes his body against mine and without conscious thought, I wrap my leg around his hip and rub myself against him like the hussy I apparently am when I'm in his company. His pheromones must block my common sense, because I always act in ways I never do when he's around. His kiss steals my breath, and his hands tangling in my hair cause a pinch of pain as he grips and tugs, holding me in place. He tears his lips away from mine and with panting breaths, trails his tongue down my throat to the V of my T-shirt and I shudder. My fingers find purchase in his hair, and I hold him in place as he licks across my exposed skin.

"So damn sweet," he mumbles against my skin.

Dropping my head back, I enjoy the sensation of his smooth tongue followed by rough bristles which send goose-bumps radiating across my body. I'm startled out of the moment when Finn pulls his mouth away suddenly and the screen door slams.

"Har—" My head snaps to the back door. "Oh, sorry. I didn't mean to interrupt anything." Stella points over her shoulder. "I'll … uh … grab your order."

By the time I have my wits about me, Stella's disappeared. I drop my leg from Finn's hip and give him an awkward smile, which possibly looks more like a grimace. "I need to grab my order." I move to step around his body, but he blocks my exit. I huff out a breath. "Can you move, please?"

"Go on a date with me."

Did he just ask me on a date? "No."

"Why not?"

"I don't need to give you a reason. Move, please."

He moves to the side and I step past him to help Stella with my order. Finn also steps outside to help bring some boxes inside, asking Stella about her produce. "Do you have a business card and a website?"

"Not a website, but I have a business card." She reaches inside her small truck and comes back to hand her card to Finn.

He takes it from her. "Thanks. I'll call you to set up a time for my head cook and me to come and see you."

Stella nods and as much as Finn started out being an asshole, I'm happy for my friend to be gaining additional business. "Stella's produce is top-notch. You won't find a better supplier."

"Thanks, Harry." Stella leaves and I stand outside awkwardly with Finn.

The moment from earlier is broken, and I'm not sure if I want to start up where we left off or pretend it didn't happen. I hitch my thumb over my shoulder toward the back door. "I need to get everything stored correctly." I spin on my heel without another word and disappear inside before Finn can respond. I lean against the cool wood of the door once it's closed and touch my fingers to my swollen lips. I don't know why I keep letting him kiss me. He's the last person I should be kissing.

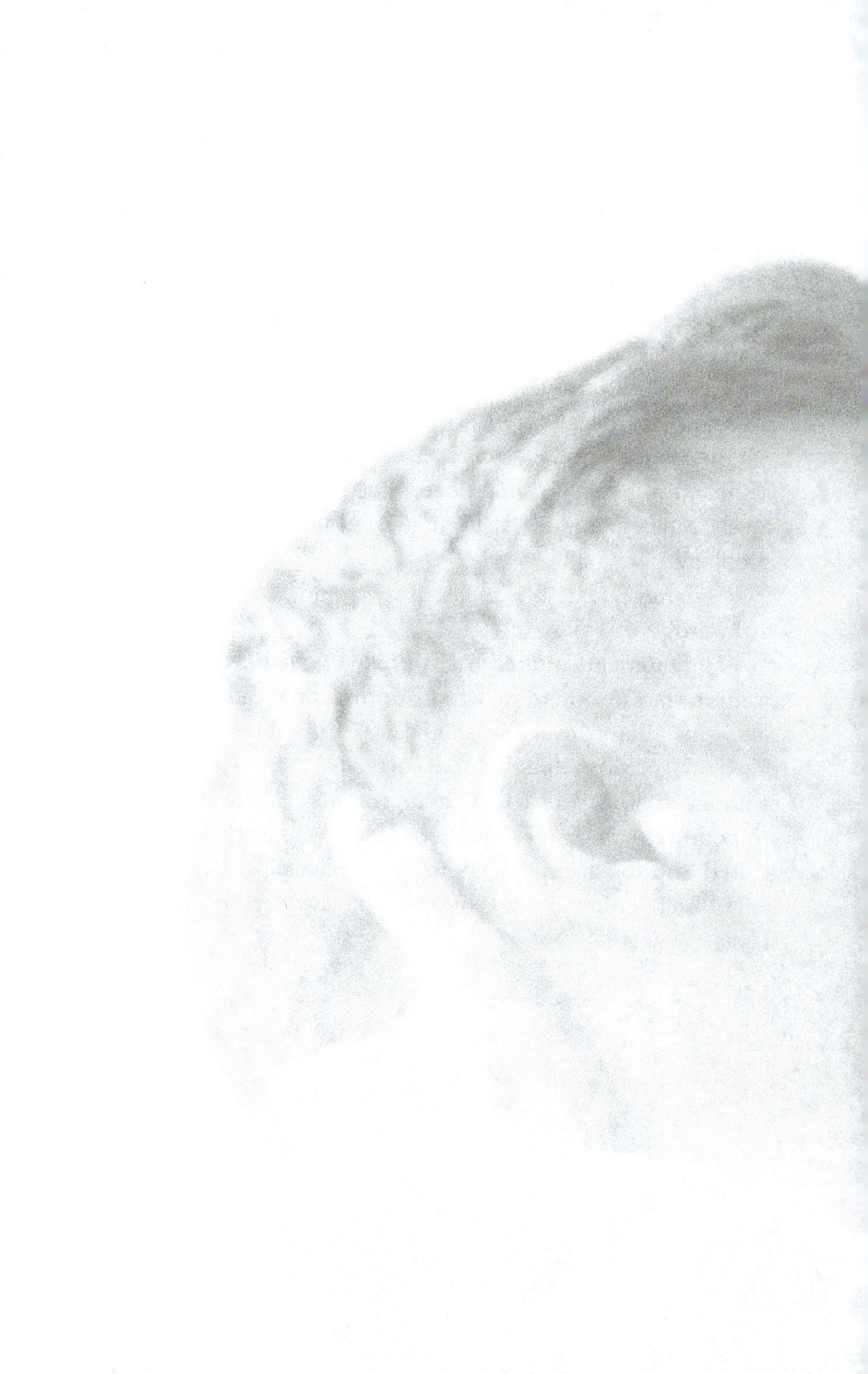

CHAPTER 10

—finn—

I ADJUST MY JEANS AS I WALK BACK TOWARD MY PUB. The challenge of getting Harry to agree to a date with me is now at the top of my to-do list. Oh, and to have my lips on hers again. I'm not sure how good my chances will be, but I'm prepared to put in the effort. It's convenient having Harry so close. I'll be able to drop in whenever I feel like it to coax her out on a date. Now I need to plan what that date will be.

I change into my soccer uniform and head through the bar. Monday nights are *my* night. That little slice of time I carve out just for me. Macy gives me a low whistle. "Nice legs!"

Several of our female patrons turn to look at me, and I wave over my shoulder as I head for the door. "Stop objectifying me," I call without turning around, then head outside to the sound of Macy's raspy laughter. I lucked out when she came knocking on my door for a job. Cocktails weren't really a thing at *Brady's*, but since she's been on board, her concoctions have certainly increased patron numbers.

I pull into the parking lot at the sports field and see Max's black Dodge Charger, so I pull into the space next to him. Grabbing my bag, I climb out of my car and lock the doors, then make my way toward my teammates and friends who are easy to spot in our team's white T-shirts. Molly is standing to the side where the guys have left their bags, so I check to see if Max is looking, then wrap my arms around Molly and land a playful kiss on top of her head.

"Hey, dickhead. Get your hands off my woman," he calls from where he's warming up.

I chuckle. "Hey, Molly."

She laughs and pushes me away for Max's benefit. "You're a shit, Finn. You love riling him up."

"Yes, yes, I do." I salute her as I jog backward to the guys, giving her my best smile. I love how protective Max is over Molly, and I'm thrilled for my friend that he's found the love of his life—even if I am a little envious of what they have. Not that I would ever tell him that.

When I get close enough, Max gives me a playful shove. "What the fuck do you think you're doing laying your hands on Molly?"

"Just saying hello. No harm in that."

Creases form between his brows. "Get your own woman."

"I'm working on it." *Shit.* I slam my mouth closed. I didn't mean to say that.

His eyebrows shoot up. Clearly, he's as surprised as I am by my statement. Placing his hands on his hips, he steps closer. "Do tell."

"Nothing to tell. I'll let you know if there's ever anything to share."

Max gives me a simple nod, then turns to the group. "C'mon. Let's do some laps to warm up."

As a group, we run a few laps, and Molly cheers us on each time we're within range. She's a great cheer squad with her over-the-top dance moves and loud praise along the sidelines. Our morale has never been so high, not that the games are serious. Monday nights are about having fun and giving us a chance to let off some steam and get a little exercise. We may trash-talk the guys on the other teams, but it's all in jest.

The final whistle blows on the teenage games and they clear the field. We do our last stretches and take up our positions. Because we change positions each week, it's my turn to step in as the goalkeeper. This should be fun. If my defenders do their job, I shouldn't have a lot to do tonight. I put on my gloves and make my way into position.

The ref blows the whistle to start the game, and it's on. The guys pass, defend, and attempt shots on goal. I do my best to defend our goal, but a ball slips past me in the sixty-third minute. I only hope our guys manage to score a second goal so we walk away winners tonight. For a bunch of guys in our thirties, we're doing okay. Lincoln runs with the ball down the wing and crosses it to Max, who kicks the ball into the top-right of the net, scoring our second goal of the game in the eighty-fifth minute. Now, I just need to make sure our opponents don't score for the next five minutes plus two minutes of injury time. Our strikers, Max and Aaron, are doing their best to keep the ball in the other half, but I'm on high alert in case the guys with their fancy mustaches break away and head toward the goal.

Finally, the ref blows the whistle three times, signaling the end of the game. I run forward to join my team as we celebrate our hard-fought win.

"Awesome job, guys. Great assist, Lincoln. And Max, that goal was perfection!" I pat both guys on the back.

We shake hands with each member of the Handlebar Mustaches and then head off the field. I don't recover as quickly as I used to, so I do a few cool-down exercises.

"Awesome job, guys," Molly says as Max wraps her in his arms and pulls her in tight. "Ewww, you're gross!" She chuckles as she playfully pushes him away.

"You love it, Dimples." Max smacks her ass, and we collect our gear to head to the parking lot.

"I'll see you guys at the pub. I'll get the pizzas started."

Thomas jogs to catch up to me. "I can't make it tonight. I have an early shift, so I'll see you next week."

"No worries, man." I slap him on the back. "Stay safe and I'll see ya next week."

Traffic is light at this time of night, so I make it back to the pub in plenty of time to get everything ready for the guys. Every Monday, after the game, the guys come back here for pizza and a couple of beers. On my way through the pub, I check that Callahan has reserved our usual tables. Not that I need to check, because he's always competent at his job. I step into the kitchen to find Miss Sylvia still working. "Why are you still here? You were supposed to finish an hour ago."

She flicks her wrist as if to erase my words. "I wanted to get these pizzas ready for the oven. I was just finishing up." She wipes her hands on her apron, then discards the soft plastic into the collection bin—we try to recycle as much as we can here.

I grab a couple of pizzas and place them in the pizza oven. When we decided Monday nights were going to be pizza nights, I immediately had a proper pizza oven installed. It was one of the best investments for the pub. Monday nights used to be dead, but now it's always packed. "Thanks, Miss Sylvia. You're the best. Now go home."

Checking the pizzas in the oven, they look ready, so I pull them out and replace them with a couple more. "Jackson, do you mind watching the rest of these and bringing them out to us?" I slide the pizzas onto the serving boards and cut them.

"No problem, Finn."

I carry the pizzas out to the main bar and slide one on each table, then take my seat at the end of the booth next to Aaron. Lincoln pushes a beer across to me and I take a long drink.

Considering I'm the owner of a pub and I spend most of my time in one, I don't drink all that much. I have the occasional whiskey with Callahan and a couple of beers on a Monday night after soccer. Dad always hammered into me it wouldn't be prudent to drink daily; he never did—unlike his father— and I respect him for that. On the other hand, Seanathair was often drunk according to the stories Dad shared about his father being a functioning alcoholic until his liver finally gave out on him. I was young when he died, so I don't remember my seanathair very well, only that he was sick and Mom used to drag me up to the hospital to visit with him while Dad was too busy with the pub.

A scuffle breaks out on the opposite side of the bar, and I shoot to my feet to sort it out. I have a zero-tolerance policy for violence of any kind in my pub. Callahan's already there, pulling Blaze away from a patron.

"What the fuck, man?" Callahan asks Blaze as he pulls him away. Blaze shoves away from Callahan and staggers haphazardly down the hallway toward the office. I tilt my head to Callahan, telling him to follow him but to keep his distance. Blaze is a big guy and can be volatile—I don't want my friend to get hurt.

The patron looks shell-shocked, and Blaze looks drunk out of his mind. "Are you okay?" I place my hand firmly on the guy's shoulder, squeezing gently to draw his attention to me and away from Blaze. Fucking Blaze has the shortest fuse of anyone I've ever met. His shift finished hours ago. Obviously, he's spent the time drinking. Something he does from time to time. I'll deal with him later, once he sobers up. My priority has to be my patron and damage control.

He turns his head to look at me as though he's only now realized I'm here. Rubbing the back of his neck, he responds, "Uh, yeah. I guess. I'm not sure what happened, though." He tilts his head to the woman standing two feet from him. "He hassled that woman, and I stepped in because she was telling him to leave her alone and he wouldn't. Then he turned on me."

"I'm sorry about that." I turn to the woman. "Are you okay, Miss?"

"He works here, right?" she snaps at me, and the guy turns his gaze back in my direction.

Shit. This could be bad for the pub. "Yes. He's my day manager and is currently off duty. So this is his time."

The woman pushes her shoulders back, and I recognize the stubborn set of her jaw. She's not going to let this go. "That doesn't make his behavior okay. He should show more respect to women and have more self-control in his position." She crosses her arms, and I have no desire to drop my gaze to her breasts as I did with Harry, even though this woman is as fired up as Harry was the first time we met. "I hope you're going to deal with him accordingly." She raises her eyebrows.

"Of course. His behavior is unacceptable. He'll be given a warning because this is the first time something like this has happened. If either of you would like to make a formal complaint, I'm happy to do that and give you each a gift card for a complimentary meal and drinks here as a small way to apologize for your negative experience." I'll be taking the money for the gift cards out of Blaze's paycheck. There's no way I'm wearing that expense when he was the damn cause.

They follow me to my office, and I complete the complaint paperwork with each of them, which is a lengthy process, but necessary. Dad set these protocols in place to ensure that our employees maintained a certain standard. It also meant that it was much easier to fire repeat offenders with a detailed paper trail—even though it's a pain in the ass. I hope it won't come to me having to fire Blaze because he is a good day manager, if not a little rough around the edges. By the time the two leave my office with their complimentary gift cards, they've exchanged phone numbers with a promise to return together to share a meal. I got the distinct vibe that things may progress between them.

By the time I return to the guys, Max, Molly, Lincoln, and Aaron are the only people left. Max frowns at me. "Everything okay?"

I drop onto the seat with a tired sigh. "Yeah. No. Not really. Fucking Blaze was causing trouble with a couple of patrons. I'm going to have to give him a warning."

"Shit, man. That's not good for business."

I nod. "I know. When he's sober, I'll talk to him."

"Sucks to be the boss," Lincoln states, and we all nod. Each of us is a boss, except for Molly.

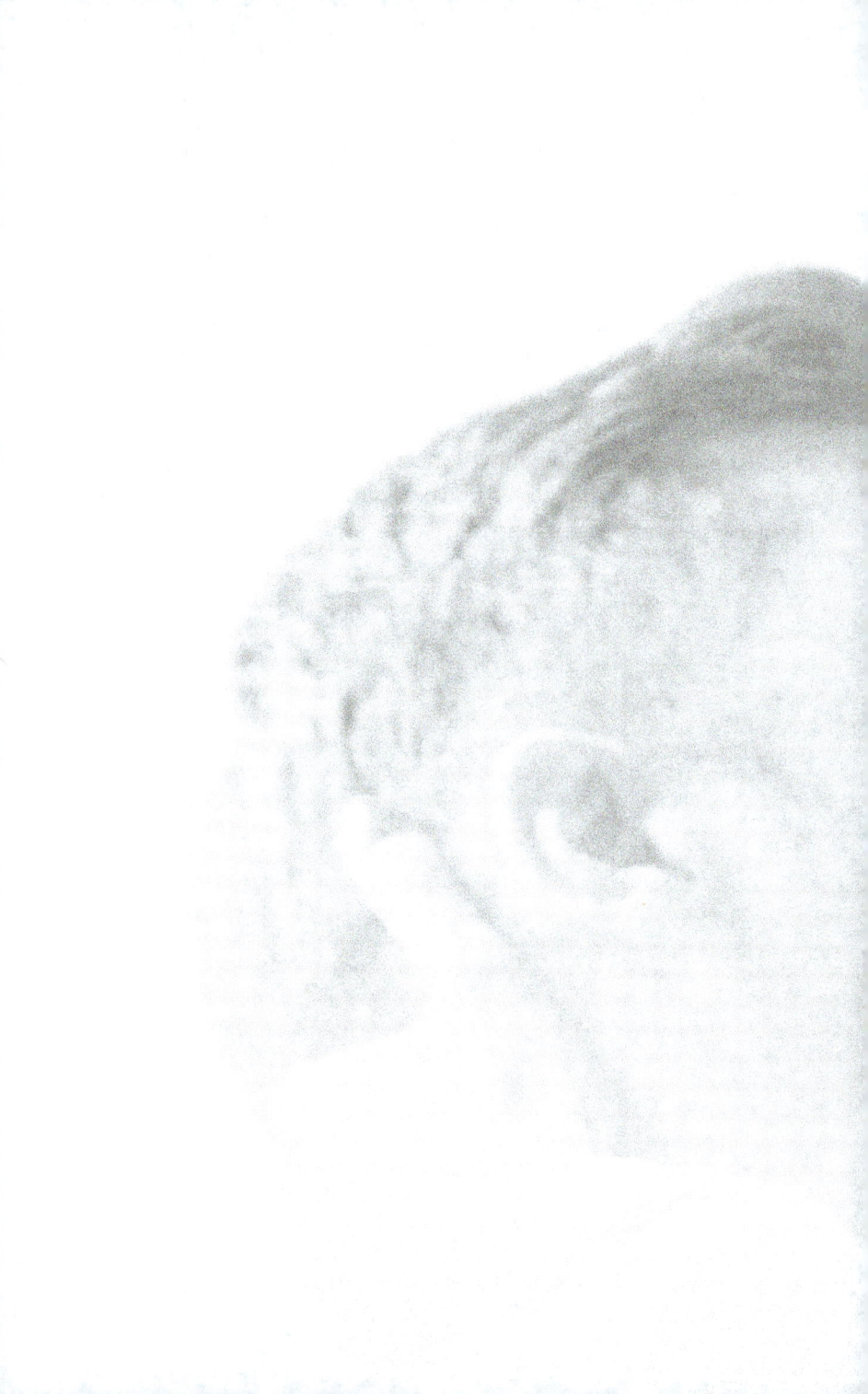

CHAPTER 11

—harriet—

I PLACE THE SPINACH AND FETA CRÊPE ON THE TABLE WITH A flourish and a smile. "Enjoy."

"Thank you. It looks divine." The young woman picks up her knife and fork, ready to dig in, and I spin on my heel to head back to the counter. As I turn around, a certain someone from next door catches my eye. His trademark sexy smirk is in place. I do my best to ignore him, but he's a customer, and I can't be outright rude to him and he knows it. This seems to be his current Monday afternoon pastime, and I'm determined to treat him with the utmost professionalism after my slip-up last week. I never should have messed with his food like that. I don't know what came over me.

That's a lie. I know exactly what came over me. My need for retribution.

Though, to be fair, since the installation of the security lights, I haven't had to deal with all the crap from that damn pub next door. I throw the building a dirty look as if I can burn it to the ground with my glare. But honestly, things have settled down on that front, which has been a blessing. I was getting tired and frustrated with the constant mess, not to mention the lack of action from the owner. I turn my glare toward Finn Brady, and my eyes zone in on his trademark smirk that pisses me off *and* sets me on fire.

Those lips. Soft and supple, yet firm and insistent.

I know exactly how they feel against mine. I bring my fingers to my lips as if the ghost of his kiss still lingers there. *What is wrong with me?* His kiss is the last thing I should think about. He notices and his lips widen, showing his perfectly straight teeth. *Damn him. Ugh!*

I turn my back on him and step behind the counter to make a double shot flat white for a customer whose body language screams *hurry up*, finishing with a genuine smile that turns hard in a split second when my eyes land on my next customer. I need to remember that he likes it when I snap at him. *Keep it professional, Harriet.*

"Welcome to *Harry's House*. What can I get for you today?" I paste on a syrupy smile.

He broadens his grin and raises his eyebrows. "So polite today, Harry. Everything okay?"

"Everything's fine."

His head snaps back and his eyes widen. "Now I know something's wrong. There's never been a time in the world's history when a woman says she's *fine* and she truly is, in fact, fine. Men everywhere know this to be fact."

I can't help it. One side of my mouth tips up before I can stop it. "Everything's fine." I hover my fingers over the iPad we use to take orders. "Now, what can I get for you?"

He looks up at the menu board. "Hmm, I'm in the mood for something sweet but a little tart today. What would you recommend?"

I narrow my eyes at him. Is he talking about me or the damn crêpe options? "Hmm, sweet *and* tart, you say." He nods emphatically, a glimmer in his gorgeous clear blue eyes. "I can recommend the strawberry apple crêpe. It's like an apple pie but in crêpe form."

"Sounds perfect. And I'll take a coffee. Shor—"

"Short black." We both speak at the same time.

"You remembered."

Damn. I shrug like it's no big deal. "It's how I take mine. It's easy to remember."

I tell him the total and he pays, stepping away to find a table.

Judy sidles up next to me as I'm preparing Finn's crêpe. "He's back, I see."

"Mhm." I don't want to give her an inch, because she'll jump on the Finn and Harry bandwagon when there's no Finn and Harry bandwagon to jump on. If she knew how many times we've kissed, she'd already be ordering wedding stationery.

"He seems to be a frequent customer."

Without looking up from my task, I answer. "It seems that way. He must like our crêpes." Well, that's what I'm telling myself, anyway.

She nudges me with her shoulder, and I glance up from loading the filling on one side of the crêpe. Her smile is cheeky and her eyes are knowing. "If you say so." She chuckles as she places Finn's coffee on the tray.

I fold the crêpe over and drizzle apple sauce over the top, finishing with a sprinkle of chopped walnuts. "Can you take this to his table?"

Judy grins at me. "Not on your life. I don't want to ruin his dining experience." She winks at me and returns to the coffee machine.

I huff, but collect the tray with Finn's order and make my way to his table through the busy space. "Your order, Sir." I carefully place his food and coffee on the table. "Will that be all?"

He studies the food carefully. "Any surprises I should know about?" He lifts his brows and studies my face intently. I feel the heat rise from my chest and make its way up to my cheeks.

The door opens and the atmosphere changes dramatically. It's instant as it sweeps across the room. I'm not the only one to notice. As I glance around, I observe several customers stiffening as they watch the doorway. I turn around to see what all the fuss is about, and my heart drops straight to my toes and through the timber floorboards. My back straightens and I swallow thickly around nothing.

"There she is!" my dad exclaims as he leans against the open door. "The inheritance thief." He points at me from across the room.

Oh my God! Finn stands from his chair, his body heat saturating my back and providing me with a modicum of comfort. I should step forward and lead my parents away from my customers before they cause more of a scene, but I'm locked in position. Finn's hand takes residence on my hip and grounds me as my parents step fully inside my café.

My pride and joy.

My grand-mère's legacy.

Their greedy eyes take in the space, and disdain overtakes their features. They were furious Grand-Mère left everything to me. They boycotted her funeral to make their point.

Finally, my feet decide to move into action, and I greet my parents. "Mom, Dad. This is a surprise." *To put it mildly.*

"I'm sure it is. I bet you were hoping we'd never step foot in here. Is this the best you could do with the old girl's money?" Dad waves his arm out and sways to the side along with the action. Everyone is watching our interaction, and I feel as though I'm one of the ants I used to study with a magnifying glass. My body heats with embarrassment and I feel a second person standing at my back. When I glance over my shoulder, I find Quentin standing with his arms crossed. His sheer size makes him a formidable-looking man. Add in the tattoos and he's downright scary.

"Mom, Dad. How about I show you the rest of the place?" Hopefully I can get them away from my patrons so they can enjoy their meals.

Mom scoffs. "I'm not interested in a tour. If this is the best you can do where it matters, I dread to see the rest."

"Get your old man a coffee." Dad waves toward the coffee machine and then staggers to the open table next to Finn's since half of my patrons have quietly crept out the door. I don't blame them; nobody likes other people's drama.

I step away from the comfort of Finn and Quentin's support and tilt my head subtly to let them know I'm okay. I'll have to think about the way Finn gave his silent support later. Finn takes his seat and Quentin reluctantly steps back into the kitchen, while I make two cups of coffee for my parents. Judy shuffles beside me.

"Are you okay?" she whispers.

I shrug. "I'm used to it. I just wish they hadn't made a scene in front of our customers. I only hope they haven't done too much damage to our reputation." I steam the milk and pour it into each cup and select two almond croissants. With shaky hands, I place the items on a tray and make my way over to my parents, smiling awkwardly at the remaining customers who witnessed the earlier scene. They return my smile with looks of sympathy. Not something I need or want.

Finn is speaking with my dad across the gap between their tables. As I get closer, I become privy to their conversation. "This is the best café around. Harry's only been open for a short time and already she has regular customers as well as customers who travel from the other side of the city especially for her crêpes and croissants. Her delicious treats and exceptional coffee are already renowned throughout the city."

My heart expands at Finn's praise, though I'm not sure how he knows any of it.

"Well, that's something at least." Dad's voice is derisive.

"It's more than something," Finn fires back. "It's everything. Places like this help to build community, and in a world like ours, where many people only think about themselves, it's important. What Harry's built here … it's everything."

I step between Finn and Dad. "Here's your coffee, and I took the liberty of choosing each of you a croissant." I turn around to face Finn and mouth, "Thank you."

He tips his head to me with a smile that's different from his usual smirk. Something passes between us and it feels … *different* somehow. Like we're on the same side.

Mom clears her throat. "Aren't you going to join us? We rarely get to see you." *And whose fault is that?*

I glance around the café, noting everyone settled with drinks and food. It's a rare moment of quiet. Damn it. Why couldn't there be a queue of people waiting to order? "I can stop for a moment, but I'll have to get up to serve."

"We can't even visit with our daughter." Mom sighs dramatically. She's good at that.

"I'm sorry. If I'd known you were going to be in town, we could have made plans for Sunday."

Dad flicks his wrist as if to wave off my suggestion. "We won't be here on the weekend. Perhaps you could take us out to dinner tonight. There's that five-star Michelin restaurant in the city."

Finn coughs behind me. "They're booked out months in advance, Dad. And I don't have the money for somewhere so extravagant. I live on a tight budget."

"What the hell did you do with all of my mom's money, Harriet?" My customers turn around to look at us since my father can't keep his voice to a reasonable level.

I scrunch my eyebrows together and chew on my lip. Dropping my voice low, I lean forward. "I'm not sure how much money you think Grand-Mère had, but after I arranged her funeral and finalized the payments to the nursing home, there wasn't all that much left. What she left in her will helped me start this café as per her instructions, but I still had to cover a lot of the expenses myself."

He huffs and he and Mom exchange a look. It's a look I'm more than familiar with. It says, *Harriet's let us down once again.* I've never lived up to their standards when they were around, which, to be fair, wasn't all that often. They left Grand-Mère to raise me for most of my childhood and teenage years. Then when it came time that Grand-Mère needed help and support, they left it up to me, which I didn't mind. She was my favorite person in the world, and I wouldn't have traded a single minute of the time I got to spend with her. As difficult as it was to watch her decline, I would do it all over again in a heartbeat.

They suddenly stand, pushing their chairs back abruptly and causing them to scrape loudly across the wooden floor. The remaining customers turn to see what's happening and I just want to shrink in on myself and hide.

"As usual, you've wasted our time today. I don't think you realize how little spare time we have, Harriet." Dad snaps as he sways. Mom reaches around to grip his elbow to steady him, but he snatches it out of her grasp and stumbles. Finn stands, coming next to me, and I wish he wasn't here to witness this. "You're always so caught up in yourself that you never think of anyone else." He takes a step toward me, stopping so close that I can smell the rancid alcohol on his breath. "You've always been a selfish child," he snarls. Spittle coating my cheek.

The backs of my eyes prick and my nose tingles, but I refuse to break down in front of them or Finn or my customers. I need to maintain some modicum of professionalism, even though my parents are bound and determined to shatter it to smithereens. I hate how small and inconsequential they still make me feel. I'm not a child anymore, dammit. I'm an adult who lets no one make me feel small or less than. I don't understand how my parents always make me revert to that helpless child who just wanted their love and affection.

Mom grips Dad's arm. "Come on, Harry. Let's go." They exit my café as quickly as they entered. I drop my head with a heavy sigh and notice their half-eaten food. So damn wasteful.

Finn's warm hand smooths up my back and settles at the base of my neck. I step forward and his hand falls away. I don't need his or anyone's comfort at this point because I'll lose the battle to keep my tears at bay. "Are you okay?"

I quickly glance at him and paste on a smile, then load the dishes left by my parents onto a tray. "I'm fine. Do you need anything?" I brave a glance at his face. His eyebrows are drawn low over his stormy eyes that have lost their playfulness from earlier. He studies my face, and I turn away to concentrate on clearing the table.

"No. I'm good. I'm more worried about you."

I force out a laugh, though I'm certain it sounds bitter. "I'm fine." I spin on my heel and head straight for the kitchen, dump the dishes, and then close myself in my tiny office. Judy and Quentin can manage for a few minutes without me. I blow out a long breath and drop my head back against the door to look up at the ceiling. The ceiling I painted myself because I wanted to save money and do the stuff I could do so I could get the coffee machine I wanted for the café. I lose the battle to hold back my tears and let them run. I've never felt more alone than I did just now. My parents have always made me feel small and unwanted, unlike Grand-Mère. Like they had no use for me. And today was no different.

"Knock, knock." Judy's voice is soft.

I wipe my face with my hands, then grab a tissue for my nose. "Can I have a minute, please?"

"Sure ... but uh ... the guy from next door wants to see you."

I don't want him to see me like this; I must look a mess. "I'll be out in a minute." More insistent knocks sound on the door. "I'll be out in a minute." I huff and pull myself together the best I can, hoping I don't look like I've just been bawling my eyes out like a child. I crack the door open and peer into the kitchen, which is empty except for Finn leaning against the stainless steel workbench in the middle of the space. The same one he trapped me against and kissed me until I was drunk on his kisses.

His usual smirk is nowhere to be seen and his normally clear blue eyes are full of concern. "Don't tell me you're okay. Because nobody would be okay after being torn down like that by their parents."

My hackles rise at the same time my chest tightens. "It's none of your business." He opens his mouth to speak and I hold up my hand to stop him. "I'm not fine right now, but I will be. I need to get back out to my customers. Thank you for checking on me, but I don't want or need your concern. I've managed just fine on my own and I'll continue to do so."

The stubborn man studies me intently for a long moment —one that feels never-ending—and I straighten under his scrutiny. He nods sharply and leaves without another word. Once he clears the doorway and I'm on my own, I blow out a long breath. My chest constricts and my stomach tightens, and I feel like a real bitch to have spoken to him like that. He was just checking on me.

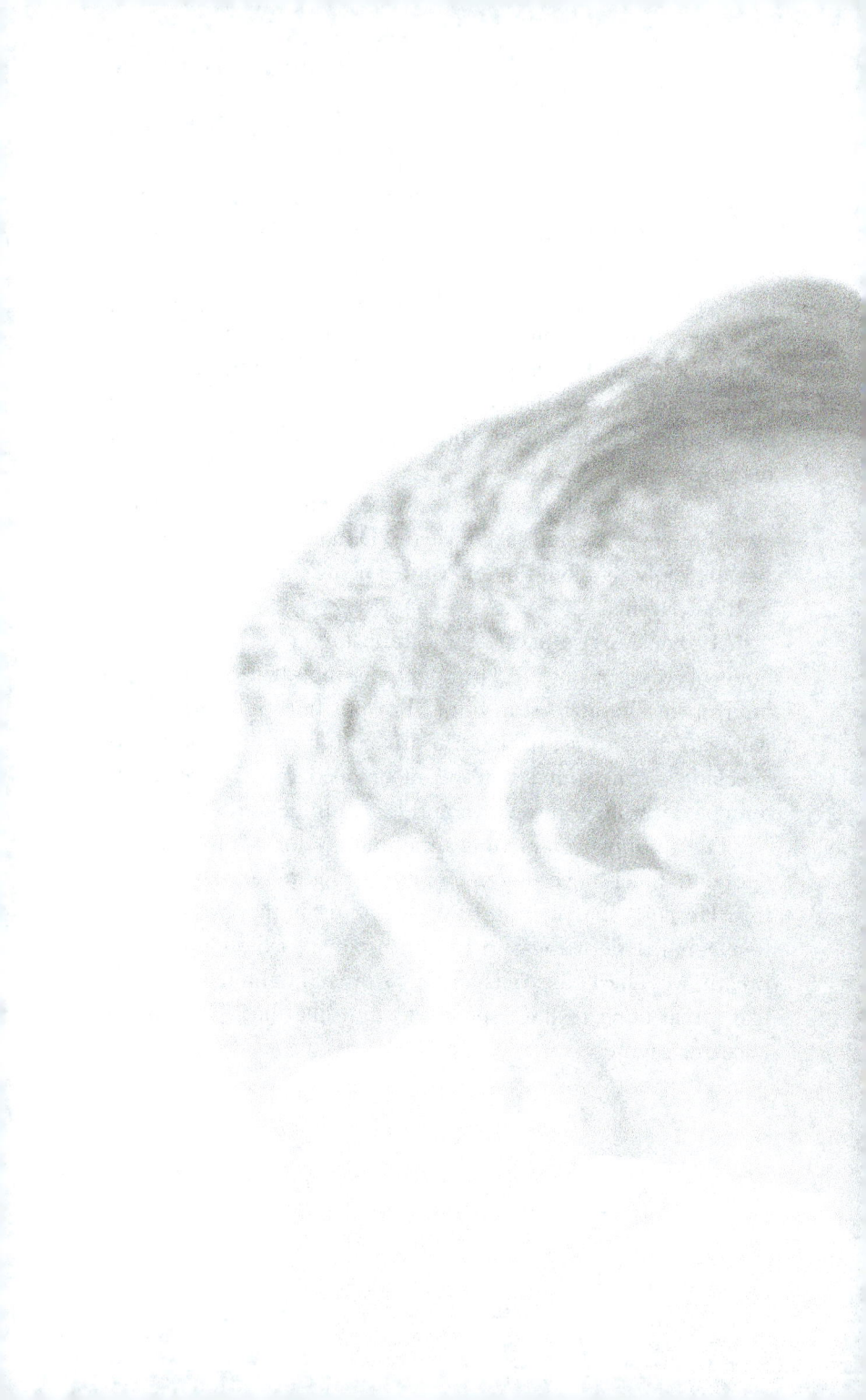

CHAPTER 12

—finn—

I HAVEN'T SEEN HARRY SINCE THE INCIDENT WITH HER PARENTS on Monday, but she's all I can think about. The woman who normally has so much fire was unrecognizable in their company. Her sparkle vanished into thin air and from the snippets of conversation I overheard, I have to wonder what her childhood was like. Her dad is obviously a functioning alcoholic; I recognize the signs a mile away. Maybe that's why she won't give me an inch. Maybe she thinks I'm into the booze too. She couldn't be more wrong, though.

Glancing at my watch, I wince at the time. Matthew will be here any minute and I haven't placed the order for fish and chips for him and his family. Stepping into the busy kitchen, Miss Sylvia, Jackson, and Layla are busy prepping for tonight's dinner service. I tuck my hands in my pockets as I prepare to be chastised for not stopping by earlier to place the order I need.

"Hey, guys." They turn and smile at me, responding with their greetings. "Uh, I'm sorry. I forgot to stop by earlier to place Matthew's order. He'll be here any minute to collect. Any chan—"

Miss Sylvia clicks her tongue. "You don't think we know the routine by now?" She points across to the fryer. "The fish is draining and the chips are almost ready."

I breathe a sigh of relief, and my lips lift as I move closer to hug the woman. "Thanks, Miss Sylvia. What would I do without you?"

She chuckles as I squeeze her tight. "You'd survive."

"I'm not so sure about that."

She pushes out of my arms and wraps the salted fish and chips in paper. It's the way they did it back in Ireland when my parents were young and we try to make the experience as authentic as possible. People come from all over for our Friday night fish and chips. I grab the bottles of soda I bought, then Miss Sylvia hands me the fish and chips, and I'm on time to meet Matthew out back.

I push through the back door and find the kid waiting for me. His face lights up as soon as his eyes land on me. "Hey." I hold up the items. "Dinner's served."

With his hands tucked in his pockets, he walks toward me with a chuckle. "Thanks, man. Good to see you."

I haven't seen him for a few days because I've been busy. "How have you been? Any luck finding work?"

He drops his head, stealing his eyes from me. "Nah. There's nothing. I've even gone door to door asking for a job. They take one look at me and say no. I might have to take you up on your offer of a haircut and some new clothes. I'm a hard worker, you know. A haircut and new clothes won't make me a better employee."

I squeeze his shoulder. "I know, Matthew. If they took the time to get to know you, they'd be offering you work like that." I click my fingers and he huffs out a deprecating laugh. "How's your mom feeling?"

He kicks the pavement with the toe of his worn sneaker, sighing. His shoulders drop, and it's almost like he folds in on himself. "The chemo's left her weak. She can barely get out of bed. I have to do everything."

"I'm sorry. I wish I could do more to help."

"Hey." Matthew and I turn toward the feminine voice. The muscle behind my ribs expands at the sight of Harry walking toward us. She's so damn gorgeous. I study her closely but find no trace of the woman I left standing in her kitchen on Monday afternoon. "I was taking out the trash when I heard you say you were looking for work." She looks directly at Matthew.

He nods and then looks down at the pavement, a blush staining his cheeks. "Uh, yeah."

"I could do with some help. It would just be waiting tables and washing dishes at this stage. Would you be happy to do that?"

Matthew snaps his head back to Harry with wide eyes. "Yeah. I'd be happy to do anything. I just need to earn some money to help support my family."

"He's a good kid, Harry. You won't be sorry."

She glances at me, then returns her attention to Matthew. "Can you start Monday at eight?"

Matthew nods eagerly. "Absolutely. Thank you so much." His smile lights his entire face and it's great to see it replace the constant worry he wears. He raises the drinks and dinner I just gave him. "Thanks, Finn. I'll be able to buy dinner now. Wow! This is amazing. Wait until I tell Mom." He spins around, his smile huge. Then he turns back suddenly. "You're serious, right? This isn't a prank or anything?"

Harry giggles and it's a tinkling sound that goes straight to my dick. "I promise I'm not pranking you." She holds out her hand and then thinks better of it, dropping it back to her side since Matthew has his hands full. "I'm Harry, by the way."

"Oh yeah, sorry. I'm Matthew." He tips his chin to her. "Is there anything I need to do?"

"You'll need to fill out some paperwork and banking details, but we can do that on Monday. You probably need to get home before your dinner goes cold." She points to the fish and chips he's holding.

"Cool. Okay, thank you." He turns toward me. "See ya on Monday." He raises the food and drink. "Thanks again for dinner, Finn."

"You're welcome." Then he's gone, disappearing around the corner of the pub.

I turn back to Harry and step closer because with her near, I can't keep my distance. I refuse to. "Thanks for helping Matthew. He's had a tough time and is trying to help his family however he can."

"You don't need to thank me. I'm happy to help. I over-heard part of your conversation about his mom and chemo." Creases form between her brows, and I reach up to smooth them away. She stiffens and steps back from me, and my hand falls to my side.

"I can pay some of his wages." Harry shakes her head. "I couldn't give him a job because of his age, so I tried to help him by providing dinner for him and his family every day. He wouldn't take money. Believe me, I've offered. He would only accept food."

Harry's posture softens. "That's kind of you to help him like that. Sometimes people just need a break." Her eyes scan me with a level of appreciation I recognize, pausing on my torso covered in my fitted gray T-shirt with the pub logo emblazoned over my left pec. Her eyes make their way back to my face. "I can afford to pay his wages. I've needed an extra pair of hands for a while now. I just hadn't gotten around to putting a sign up in the window. I even have the paperwork he'll need to complete in my office." She shrugs.

"He'll work hard. He's been looking for work for a while,

but nobody will hire a kid who looks homeless. I offered to buy him some new clothes, but he wouldn't accept it."

"I have no doubt. Maybe I'll get him a couple of pairs of pants and some T-shirts as a uniform. What size do you think he'd be?"

I step back into her space and slide my fingers through her silky hair, tucking the curly strands behind her ear. She doesn't pull away this time and I mentally fist bump. "You don't have to do that. I can buy him a uniform." I glance at the time. "Or we could buy them together. We could go to Target now if you have time."

"Oh, um." She points over her shoulder toward her building. "I was just finishing a deep clean of the fridge. I'm not quite finished."

I shrug. "I can wait. Come and grab me when you're finished." That'll give me time to let the staff know I'll be out for a while and maybe I can convince her to have dinner with me. Something casual.

"Uh, sure."

Forty minutes later, we're pulling into the nearest mall with a Target. We make our way through the store and head straight for the menswear section. "What type of clothes do you want to get for Matthew?"

She bites her bottom lip. "I don't know. I hadn't thought about it. Maybe some black cargo pants and a couple of polo shirts. There was an embroidery place on the way in. I could get my logo stitched onto the shirts and pants. I might even get myself and Judy fresh shirts. That way, Matthew won't see it as a handout."

"Good idea." I collect Harry's hand in mine and lead her

toward the cargo pants. She doesn't balk when I tangle my fingers with hers. The only problem is that we need to separate when we get to the pants and need to search for the correct size.

"What size do you think he is?"

"He's about the same size I was at his age." I search through the racks and find a pair of black pants in a size I've long since left behind. "These should do the trick." I hand them to Harry and search for another pair the same size. We then head over to the polo shirts. "What color shirts do you want to get him?"

"I'd like to say white, but white will probably get too dirty."

"Will he be wearing an apron?"

"Yeah, probably."

I shrug. "That'll probably help keep the shirt clean."

She smiles at me and my insides flip. "True."

We grab a couple of white polo shirts in Matthew's size, then grab a couple of women's shirts and head straight to the checkout. I take Harry's hand in mine again, enjoying the feel of her small fingers entwined between mine and study her as she makes a beeline for the front of the store.

She glances up at me. "What?"

"Nothing."

"Why are you looking at me like that?"

"Like what?" I grin at her with a wink.

"I don't know. Like you've never seen a woman before." She chuckles, and it hits me right in the solar plexus. "Oh, maybe we should get him some non-slip shoes, too."

"Smart."

I have to guess his size when we divert to the men's shoe section. We settle on a pair that may be slightly too big, but it's better to be safe than sorry, then head to the front of the store. We arrive at the checkout and Harry's attention diverts to the lady behind the register. I have my credit card ready to scan as soon as the last item is processed. "What are you doing?"

"Paying. I thought that was obvious."

"He's going to be *my* employee. I can do this."

I guide Harry out of the store with my hand on the back of her neck. "I know you can, but I wanted to help. It's the least I can do."

Thankfully, she drops it and I slide my hand down her arm to take her hand again. I like this. The simplicity of holding her hand. We head to the embroidery kiosk and Harry leaves the clothes to be embroidered with her café's logo.

"The man said it'll take about an hour." Perfect.

"We can wander while we wait."

"Don't you need to get back to the pub? I can find my way back to the café."

"No way. I have time." I spot a sushi bar and my stomach growls.

Harry chuckles and raises her brows. "Hungry?"

"Yeah. Mind if we stop for something to eat?"

"Can't you eat at work?"

"When I eat at work, I get interrupted. It'd be nice to eat a meal in peace for once."

Her shoulders drop and the stiffness disappears from across her shoulders. "I didn't think about what it must be like to run a pub. We can eat here. I'm a little hungry myself."

I feel as though I've just made a monumental step forward with Harry. Without wasting a second, I tug her forward and ask the hostess for a table. I want to speak with Harry about her parents and the things they said on Monday, but I don't want to send her running in the opposite direction when I feel like she's beginning to soften toward me.

We take our seats and each of us takes a plate of sushi from the conveyor belt. We're both quiet as we take our first bites of food. I rarely have a problem striking up a conversation. I am a publican after all so I'll talk to anyone. It's part of my DNA. But I don't know how to start the conversation I want to have with Harry.

Harry swallows the last bite of her chicken teriyaki roll, then locks her gaze on me. "What's it like to own a pub?"

I'm relieved she's the one who broke the ice. "I'm the second generation to own Brady's and before that, my seanathair owned a pub back in Ireland."

Her eyes widen. "Oh, wow. That's some legacy."

I nod. "It's a lot of pressure, if I'm honest. Dad still stops by from time to time to tell me what I'm doing wrong. But he means well. He dedicated most of his life to the pub, so it'd be hard for him to let it go completely."

Harry covers my hand and gently squeezes. I flip my hand over to tangle my fingers with hers. "That'd be tough. Parental judgment can be hard."

Here's my opening. "How are you feeling after the visit from your parents on Monday?"

She blows out a heavy breath and focuses on the conveyor belt, then grabs a plate of wakame, so I collect a plate of tomago nigiri, worried that she's going to clam up. "I'm sorry you and everyone else had to witness my parents. I don't know how I manage, but I always seem to forget how toxic they are. They've always been like that. Thankfully, they traveled a lot with my dad's work, so I spent most of my time with my grand-mère." A smile touches her kissable lips. "She gave me my love for French treats. We spent many hours in her kitchen making delicately flakey croissants and beautifully light crêpes."

"Sounds like you were close."

Her face softens, taking on a wistful look. "Yeah, we were. It was hard in her final years when I had to watch her memories fade. She didn't remember me or the times we shared. She thought I was a sweet stranger who'd spend time with her occasionally, even though I visited with her every day." I tighten my fingers around hers, and she lifts a delicate shoulder. "I knew it was inevitable, so I tried not to take it personally."

We're both quiet for a few moments. "I can't imagine how difficult that was for you."

"She's the reason I opened the café. I wanted to honor her memory. It was something we used to talk about doing together one day."

I reach over and stroke my hand down her cheek, and she leans into my touch. "She'd be proud of what you've built in a short time."

Her lips tip up. "Yeah. I think she's watching over me." This close, I can see the various shades of green that make up her eyes. I can also see the happiness as well as a tinge of sadness shimmering within their depths.

We finish eating, then I pay for dinner and congratulate myself on taking Harry on a pseudo date without her realizing it. Harry grabs the uniforms and we head back to the pub as the sun kisses the horizon. As I turn off the engine, my heart stutters that our time together has ended unless I can coax her to come in for a drink.

"Did you want to come in for a drink?" I ask as we both climb out of my car.

Harry glances at the pub, then back to me. "Sorry. I need to finish my prep for the morning, then I should get home. I have an early start."

"Oh right, fair enough." I walk to the back of the car to meet Harry halfway. "Thanks for giving Matthew a chance. I know he won't let you down."

"No problem. Matthew and I will both benefit from the arrangement."

I step closer and cup Harry's face, then slide my fingers into her curls and tilt her face up to mine. I scan her delicate features in the near darkness. She swallows and licks her lips, and I can't hold back any longer. I touch my lips to hers in a barely there press. She pushes up onto her toes and our mouths come together, making full contact. I drop my other hand to her hip and pull her tight to my body as I swipe my tongue across her lips with a groan. Harry moans and wraps her arms around my neck, tangling her fingers in my hair, making my heart skip a beat. Her short nails scrape my scalp, sending sparks racing through my body. My cock decides it's time to come out to play and rises to attention, filling my pants. I press my groin against Harry's stomach and nip her bottom lip with my teeth. As she moans, I take the opportunity to slide inside, to taste her. Harry isn't a passive participant in the kiss. She gives as good as she gets. Our tongues explore and our breaths mingle together with her sighs and my moans.

The sound of glass bottles clanking on the pavement tears us apart, and I scan the parking lot, but we're alone. If someone was out here, they're gone now. I glance down at Harry's gorgeous face and have to assume her cheeks are flushed from our kiss since it's dark now. She takes a step back and I reluctantly let her go.

"I ... uh ... should finish up so I can get home." She bends down to pick up her shopping. "Thanks for this and for dinner. It was ... really nice." Pressing up on her toes, she lays a light peck on my bristly cheek, and I feel it all the way to my soul. It's innocent in its nature, yet it means so much coming from Harry.

"I'll walk you across the alley." I take the shopping from her and tangle my fingers with hers.

She smiles up at me as we walk, her security lights coming on as we get close to her building. "Thanks, Finn. For everything. I'll ... um ... I'll see you when I see you."

Resting my hand above Harry on the doorframe, I press in close and lower my head to take another kiss. I don't want our evening to end, but if it has to, then I want more kisses to hold me over. We pick up where we left off, and our kiss goes from zero to one hundred in mere seconds. By the time we pull apart, we're both breathing heavily into the night air.

I kiss her forehead, my lips lingering for a moment. "Goodnight, Harry." I step away from her, tuck my hands in my pockets, and watch her fumble with the lock.

She glances over her shoulder. "Night, Finn." Then she disappears inside.

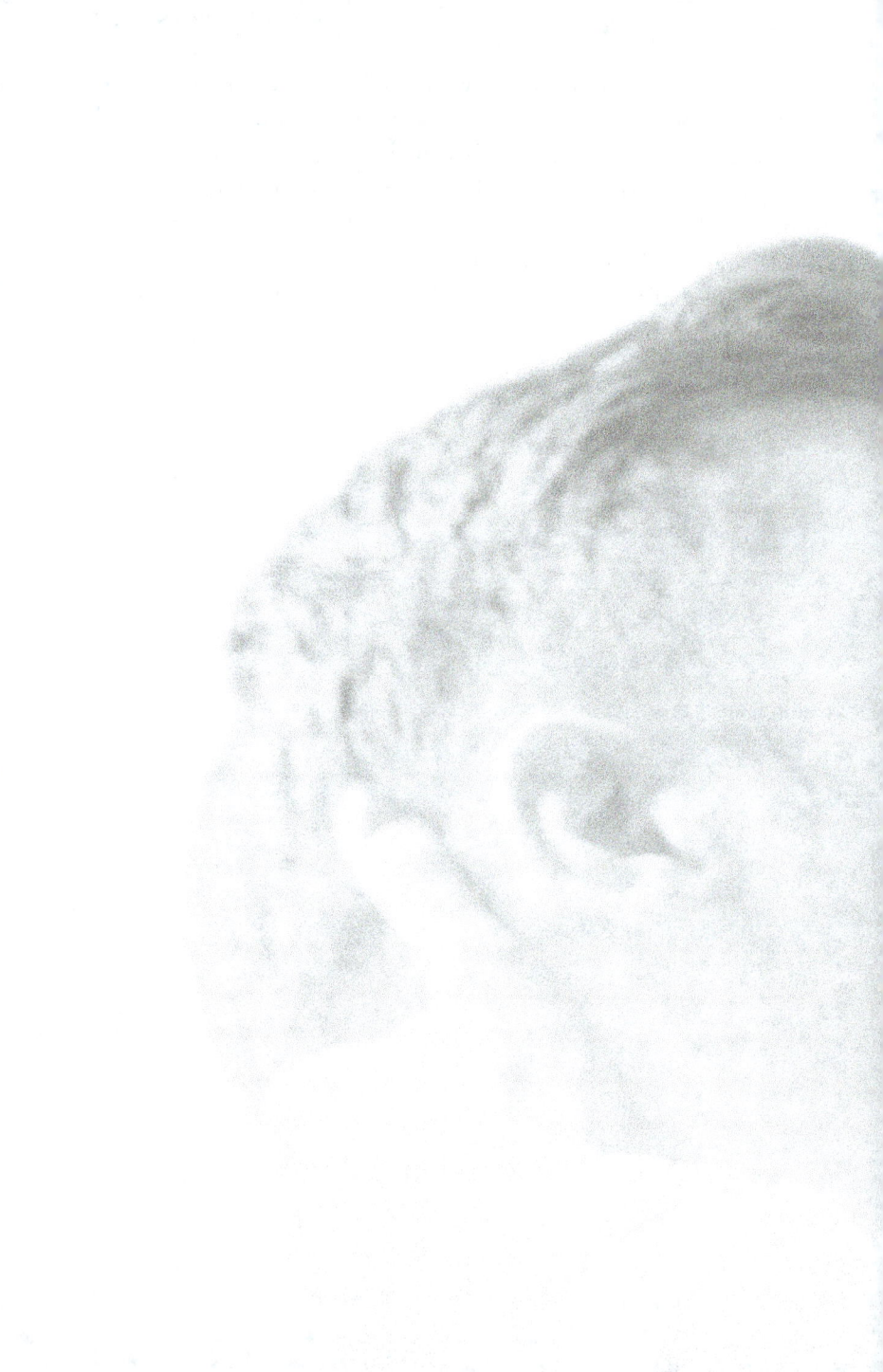

—harriet—

I BLOW OUT A LONG BREATH AS I DROP INTO MY OFFICE CHAIR. Every day seems busier than the last, and I'm not about to complain, but it's exhausting. Thank goodness I found Matthew. While he waits tables, Judy assists me behind the counter. Some days, we even get the opportunity to take a break. Most days, though, I don't seem to stop from the minute I walk in here until I walk out in the late afternoon. It's a long-ass day. But the business is doing amazing—beyond my wildest dreams.

"Knock. Knock."

I head straight for the back door to greet Stella, adjusting my ponytail on the way. "Hey."

"Hey." She points behind her. "I had to park down the street today."

I step outside. "How come?" As we walk to the side of my building, the reason comes into view. A black truck on giant wheels is parked in the alleyway between my café and *Brady's Pub*. I've seen the truck in the parking lot behind the pub, so I'm assuming it belongs to someone who works there. Maybe they had to pick something up and unload it and haven't had time to move it yet. "Right. That would definitely make it hard to get through. I guess we'll be giving our muscles a workout today."

Stella chuckles. "I guess so." We head down the street and grab a box each and make our way back to my café. We have to repeat the process several times, and by the time we're done, we're both sweaty and exhausted.

"Come in. I'll make you an iced tea before you head off. I feel terrible that you had to park so far away today. Hopefully, it won't happen again."

She waves off my concern. "It's not a problem, but I'll take the iced tea. Mind if I wash my hands?"

"Go for it." I wash mine, then set about making iced tea for myself and Stella, and we sit at my stainless steel counter to drink it.

"So, how are things going with the sexy pub owner next door?"

I almost choke on the tea I was about to swallow and Stella jumps up from her stool to pat my back. "Okay, I guess. Has he come down to check out your business?"

"Yeah. He brought his head cook with him. She's so sweet and was super impressed with my setup. They'll probably switch to me in around six weeks when their other contract ends."

I squeal in delight. "I'm so happy for you."

She smiles. "Yeah, me too. Going organic has been a lot of hard work, and it was an enormous risk, but it's paying off." Stella tips up her drink, finishing her iced tea. "Anyway, I need to keep moving. Thanks for the drink and the chat."

I walk Stella out, noting the obnoxious truck still parked in the alleyway.

It's still there when Liam delivers my dairy products and eggs, meaning we have to lug crates farther than we really should. All I can do is apologize with each trip we make back to his truck.

The last ten days have been like groundhog day. The obnoxious truck has blocked the alleyway each afternoon and is gone once we complete all of my deliveries. I figured it was a one-off thing the first day, and then shrugged it off the day after that, but this is ridiculous. I thought we'd turned a corner and were sort of … *friends*. I had hoped that this type of behavior was a thing of the past. Maybe I shouldn't expect so much from my business neighbor. Once an inconsiderate asshole, always an inconsiderate asshole, I guess. I know it's not his truck, but still.

After the third day, I started taking photos and I plan to confront Mr. Brady with the evidence of this latest transgression. I check I have the photos in the folder on my phone labeled *Brady's Pub*. Each one clearly shows the date and time of day in the information, so there can be no denying it. I'm not bothering with an email this time. I need to deal with this face-to-face.

Not because I want to see him. Well, that's what I'm telling myself.

I drop my phone back into my cross-body purse, take a calming breath, grip the long brass handle on the heavy wooden door, and drag it open. Pausing inside, I take a moment to allow my eyes to adjust to the dimness, then make my way across the mosaic-tiled floor to the beautiful timber bar, which looks old but well-kept. Green pendant lights hang from the ornate ceiling, and groups of polished wooden tables and chairs decorate the space. It's classy, which wasn't what I was expecting to find when I first came here months ago looking for the owner. A woman who looks remarkably like Gal Gadot pops up from behind the bar—a towel draped over her left shoulder—and greets me with a warm smile. She's stunning.

"Welcome to *Brady's*. What can I get for you?"

I'm taken aback by her friendliness, but I guess she doesn't know I'm the business owner next door and that I've had words with her boss. I glance down at her name badge. "Uh, hi, Macy. I was hoping to speak with Mr. Brady."

"You mean Finn?"

"Yes, please." I glance around, noting there are several customers in booths along the side of the room. There's an arched opening to another space and on the other side, there's a hallway. "Is he available?"

She raises a single eyebrow, crosses her arms, and looks me up and down. "Why do you need to see him?"

I point next door. "I'm Harry from next door." As if that explains exactly why I need to see him.

Her eyebrows shoot up and a slow smile crawls across her lips. "Riiight. Harry. Well, that explains a couple of things." A customer steps up to the bar and Macy holds up a finger to me and then serves him, leaving me completely confused. "I'll check if he's available. Would you like a drink while you wait?"

"No thanks. I'm okay."

"Suit yourself." She steps out from behind the bar and disappears down the hallway. I fidget where I stand, not sure if I should take a seat at the bar or move closer to the hallway. I decide to move closer to the hallway. After a few minutes, Macy steps out from what I presume is Finn's office with the infuriating man wearing a furrow between his brows and what appears to be a sports uniform close behind. When he notices me, the furrow disappears and is replaced by his usual smug smirk. Like he thinks I'm here to see *him*.

Well, I am, but not because I find him insanely attractive and wanted to see him. Not at all.

Macy steps past me, her perfume wafting behind her, and I follow her with my eyes as she heads back to the bar. She's so damn attractive … and so tall. Her legs go on for miles. I wonder if she and Finn … *Stop it.* It's not your business and definitely has no bearing on the reason you're here.

Finn comes to a stop in front of me. I mean he stops *inside* my personal bubble and ordinarily, I'd take a step back if someone came so close to me, but for some reason, I don't. What's the point after the heated kisses we've already shared? It's infuriating how attractive I find the man. He tilts his chin down and I tip my head back. "Harry," he breathes, his voice full of disbelief. "Welcome to *Brady's*. It's good to see you." He leans in to kiss my cheek in welcome, but I withdraw in time to avoid his lips. I can't have his lips anywhere near me or I'll forget why I've come here. He quickly replaces the frown from my withdrawal with a smile and gestures toward the room he came from. "Come into my office, Firecracker. We can speak in private."

I take the first step toward his office, and butterflies erupt in my stomach. The last few times we've been alone, I've ended up trapped against something and kissed like I was the very air he needs to breathe. Worse still, I *liked* it.

More than I should.

Is that *why* I came here instead of emailing?

Do I *want* Finn to kiss me again?

Shit. Is that what I want?

We step over the threshold and when Finn closes the door with a click, silence descends and I'm worried he'll hear the heavy beat of my heart as it hammers against my ribs. Suddenly, I can't quite remember why I came over here. And maybe I shouldn't have followed him so easily into a confined space.

He walks further into his office. "Would you like a drink?" Stopping at a small fridge built into the cupboard, he opens it. "Water, juice, soda?"

Maybe a drink would be a good idea. My mouth is as dry as the Mojave Desert. "Water would be great, thanks."

He hands me a bottle of water, and our fingers make brief contact, adding to the riot of sensations running through my body. Finn grabs one for himself and tips his head back, taking a long drink. I quickly open mine and take a drink—hoping it soothes my nerves—and dig deep, looking for my anger to replace my sudden bout of lust.

"So, you wanted to see me? Is everything okay with Matthew?" The water goes down the wrong pipe, and I choke. How did he know I wanted to see him? Am I that obvious? "It must be important for you to come in person, or did you miss me?" That sexy smirk of his makes an appearance, and my blood heats. I'm unsure whether it's because it reminds me of the first time we met or how much I hate that I'm attracted to the man. Either way, it's a positive because it reminds me why I'm here.

I calmly place the bottle of water on the corner of his desk and stand to my full height, which still leaves me at a pitiful disadvantage. He's so freaking tall. Well, most people are tall compared to me, so maybe he's not quite *that* tall. "Matthew's working out great. He's settled in quickly and is proving to be a real asset. Quentin's even taken him under his wing and is teaching him how to make croissants."

Finn nods along, smiling. "I'm really happy to hear that. He's stopped by a couple of times to tell me how much he loves it."

Oh, that's great to know. "I'm glad he's enjoying it." And there I go, getting derailed from the reason I came here. "I'm here about another business-related issue." I try to fill my tone with as much controlled professionalism as I can.

He takes a step closer. "Of course you are." That knowing look has returned to his eyes, and I narrow mine.

"What do you mean by that?"

He moves closer still. "If it was a business-related issue, you could have emailed. You're good at those."

My hackles rise. I thought we'd turned a corner in our relationship, but clearly, I was wrong. He thinks he knows me so well and dammit, he's right. I spin on my heel and head for the door, filling my voice with as much disdain as I can. "Fine, I'll head back and shoot you an email. I expect a more professional response this time." My hand connects with the cool metal of the handle and Finn's front connects with my back. *Wow!* He moves fast. My heart pounds as my chest presses against the smooth surface of the wood. He burrows his face into the crook of my neck, drawing in my scent, then rubs his scruff along my sensitive flesh until his mouth is right next to my ear.

His warm breath whispers across my skin with his words. "Don't be like that, Firecracker."

My breaths come in short pants, and I'm worried I'm about to hyperventilate with his proximity. He presses his whole body against mine, and there's no mistaking he's turned on.

That makes two of us.

A wanton moan escapes my lips without permission and I close my eyes in embarrassment as I press my thighs together, trying to stem the instant ache he's created in my body. He sucks in a sharp breath. *What the hell is wrong with me?* Whenever he's around, my body goes haywire and I have no rational explanation. Sure, I find Finn attractive. But this isn't me. I press back into his groin and he wraps one arm around my middle, holding me tight to him, his heavy breaths teasing me in between open-mouthed kisses. Tilting my head to the side, I give him easier access and he doesn't hesitate to suck on my pulse point, sending my blood thrumming through my veins.

"You like my mouth on you. Admit it."

Turning my head to the side, I lock eyes with Finn's stormy blue irises, which are quickly being swallowed by his pupils. "Never." He pushes into my body harder, trapping me against the door, and I swear to God that my nipples are trying their best to drill through the wood. Against my better judgment, I don't struggle to get free. Finn traces my face with his eyes, then he drops his gaze to my lips. I'm not sure if I move, but he presses his lips roughly to mine, and I match his intensity. Our teeth collide as our tongues tangle for dominance. Tasting copper on my tongue, I realize I've inadvertently bitten him. He snaps his head away from me and swipes his tongue across his bottom lip, cleaning away the evidence of my aggression.

His lips tip up, and he raises a single brow. "I love your fire." Simultaneously, he slides his hand lower, connecting with my needy clit through my cotton skirt, making me moan. "Fuck, I can feel how hot you are through your skirt. Tell me I can touch you." I press my lips together. "Don't think about it. *Feel* it." He swipes the throbbing bundle with his fingers and I push into his touch. "Your body wants me, whether or not your mind is on board. Tell me what I want to hear, Harry."

I capture his lips with mine, hoping my kiss conveys the permission I refuse to give with words. I want his hands on me, but the rational side of my brain says I shouldn't be giving in so easily. This girl is not me. I've never been this girl. Nobody else has ever made me this desperate.

Why did it have to be him?

He nips at my lip and then pulls away. His breaths are choppy and his eyes are dark as they pierce mine. He drags his hand away from where I want it most, and I grip his wrist to hold him in place. "I need your words, Firecracker. Don't hold out on me now." One side of his mouth tips up and he raises an eyebrow as he pushes his hardness against my hip.

Swallowing my pride, I nod. "Touch me," I murmur, too turned on to go back now.

"Tsk. Tsk. Tsk." He pauses. "Manners," he chastises me and my hackles rise.

I push against him, some of my senses coming back to me. "This is a terrible idea. I don't know how I always end up in this situation with you. You arrogant ass." He chuckles and his breath fans across my face while he moves slightly, so I'm completely sandwiched between his firm body and the door. I should feel scared, or at the very least, nervous, but I feel neither of those things. His dominance is turning me on more than I've been turned on in ... well, I don't think I've ever been this turned on. I know if I were to say no or stop, he would. That's the weird thing. I trust Finn completely. Even though he comes across as arrogant, he's never come across as a guy who would take advantage of a woman. "C'mon, Harry. One little word and I'll put us both out of our misery." He nips me where my neck meets my shoulder, then licks his way up to my ear. "Please," he whispers.

Blowing out a breath, I can't believe I'm about to give in, but I have the biggest case of blue lady balls and I'd be stupid to turn down what he's offering when I know it'll be good. Probably better than good. God, how big will his head be if he manages to make me orgasm? I lock eyes with him, gritting my teeth. "Plea—"

He smashes his lips to mine, spinning my body and pressing my back against the door in one swift action before I can finish the word. Our kiss is hungry, with underlying aggression. His tongue invades my mouth and dominates me in the same way as his body does. I wrap my arms around his neck and his hands cup my ass to lift me, pressing my clit against the bulge in his shorts. I rub myself against him, creating beautiful friction and taking what I need. One at a time, Finn moves each hand, sliding it along my thigh, until he's gripping my ass without the pesky fabric in the way, his long fingers slipping beneath the satin of my soaked panties, and I push down. My heart's pounding and with our chests pressed together, I can't miss his matching erratic rhythm.

"You're fucking drenched for me," he murmurs in my ear —his voice ragged.

His fingers glide through my slit and push into my opening without preamble, and a long moan escapes from the deepest part of me. I drop my head back against the door, closing my eyes to enjoy the sensations. My mind is free of everything except for Finn. I'm surrounded by him—my senses are full of his scent, taste, and touch. Sliding his fingers roughly in and out of me, his mouth consumes mine, mimicking his fingers. Using my thighs wrapped around his slim hips, I match his movements, pushing down to take him deep, chasing the high that's building rapidly.

He tears his lips away and rubs his scruff along the side of my cheek until he reaches my ear. His warm breath sends goosebumps racing across my heated flesh. "Give me what I want, Harry. I need you to come all over my fingers." His words rumble through me and the sparks that were growing, expand and overwhelm me as I push down on Finn's fingers, rubbing my clit against his erection in a frenzy. "That's it. Take what you need to give me what I want," he grunts.

My mouth falls open as I tighten and pulse around his fingers. His mouth quickly covers mine, and he swallows my cry of euphoria while my body shudders with my release. *Holy shit.* The man has magic fingers. And mouth. And tongue. I bet it'd feel amazing with his mouth included in the action on my lady parts. Lord only knows how smug he's bound to be after making me come so fast. I peel my eyes open when he stops kissing me to find him studying my face. "You're fucking glorious when you come." He carries me over to his desk and sits me on the cool surface, then gives me a short, hard kiss.

With his hand resting on my hip, he slides open the top drawer and shuffles things around. Slamming it closed, he repeats the process with the next drawer down with a curse.

"What are you looking for?"

"A damn condom." *Oh.* Makes sense, I guess. I hadn't even thought about protection. I'm glad at least one of us still has some sensibilities left. I guess it's a good sign that he didn't have a condom on hand. It means he doesn't fuck women here on the regular. He holds up a finger. "Stay there. I'll be right back." It's a demand, not a request.

He escapes out the door, and I take a moment to study his office. It's all dark wood, much like the bar out front. I trace the surface of his desk, and now that the lust has cleared somewhat, the reasonable side of my brain reengages.

What the hell did I just let him do to me?

Why did I do that?

He's an asshole, and I let him finger me, and worse than that, I rubbed myself all over him like a wanton hussy. I gave him something I normally keep sacred—my orgasm face. I don't let just anybody see my orgasm face. Mortification fills me rapidly, and I hop down from his desk, adjusting my skirt and soaked panties. I pull my top back into place so I don't look like I just had the most mind-blowing orgasm of my life and make my way toward the door.

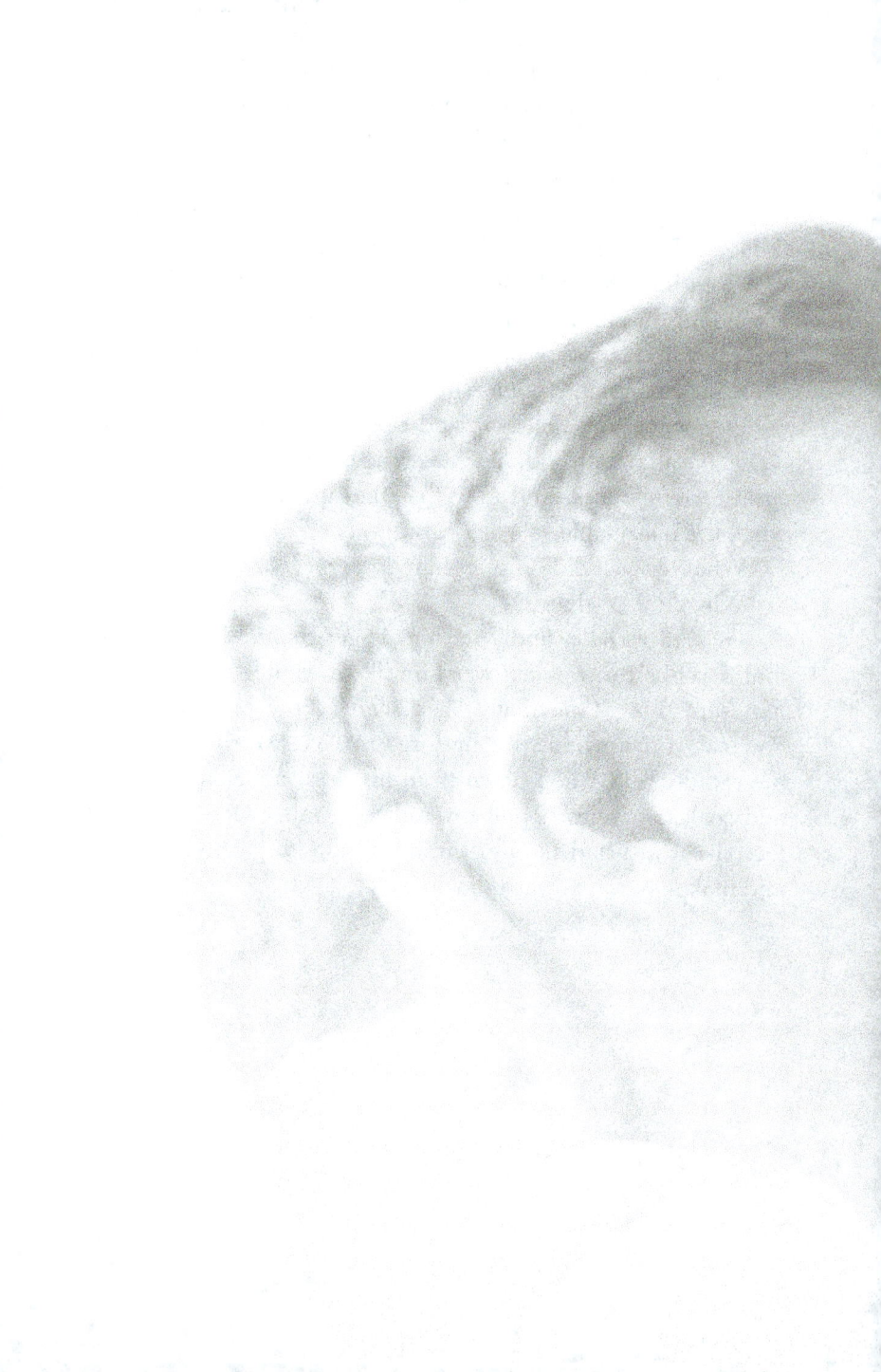

CHAPTER 14

—finn—

I CAN'T BELIEVE I DON'T HAVE ANY CONDOMS IN MY OFFICE, not that I fuck women there. No. Harry would be the first for that. My mouth tips up at the visual of her coming all over my fingers. I load the coins into the machine in the men's bathroom and grab the package, then spin on my heel to return to the sexy as fuck woman currently waiting for me on my desk. I adjust my cock in my shorts. I'll probably be late for soccer, but I don't care. Barging through the door, I almost knock Harry on her ass. Narrowing my eyes, I stalk forward. "Where do you think you're going?" *Has she come to her senses?*

She juts her chin in the air. "Home."

I close the door behind me and engage the lock. Her eyes follow the action and her throat moves as she swallows. I'll let her go if that's what she wants, but I'd rather finish what we started. If I'd had a damn condom in my drawer, I'd already be balls deep inside her by now, not preparing to get her head—and body—back in the game. I'm up for the challenge, though. She moves toward the door and I reach up and cup the side of her jaw, my thumb pressing against her plump bottom lip.

Leaning forward, I replace my thumb with my lips. A tender kiss that's so different from the kisses we've already shared.

"Stay. I'll make it worth your while," I whisper hopefully.

Indecision filters across her face, and she tucks her bottom lip behind her teeth. "I really should go. That shouldn't have happened." She points at the door and her pupils dilate. When I glance down, the pulse point at the base of her throat is fluttering a fast rhythm. She may say that it shouldn't have happened, but she loved every minute. I could tell by the way she was riding my fingers and rubbing against my cock. *Do I let her go or do I try to convince her to stay?*

I drop my hand to her hip and squeeze. Indecision filters across her face, but she takes a small step closer. Her breasts press against my body and her hand drops to my heavy cock. Palming it, she presses up on her toes and runs her tongue across my bottom lip. "I guess it's only fair for me to return the favor. I'd hate to leave you with blue balls," she murmurs.

"Are you sure?" I have to ask. I don't want to force her. That's not my style.

She nods. "I'm sure."

Wasting no time, I pick her up and carry her back to my desk. "Take off your panties."

Her pupils dilate, and she wastes no time dropping her panties to the floor. I bend down and scoop them up, taking a long sniff, then glide my hand slowly up the inside of her smooth leg until I reach her pussy. Her heat welcomes me before I reach the apex of her thighs, and she widens her legs to give me better access. *That's it.* Her hand grips my hair as I push her skirt past her hips, getting my first look at her pussy.

Groaning, I drop to my knees and run my nose along her slit, then rub her clit. Her musky scent fills my nose, and I draw it deep into my lungs. Her grip on my hair tightens when I replace my nose with my tongue, and a tiny moan escapes her lips. When I look up, I find her eyes locked on me and my cock grows heavy. *That's so hot.* So many women shy away from eye contact during sex, but Harry's full of fire, and I get the impression she doesn't shy away from anything. She pushes her hips to the edge of the desk, and I stroke her slit with my tongue and then drag my fingers through her folds until I reach her opening. She's still so fucking wet and swollen for me.

I push my middle finger into her heat, then quickly replace it with two, ensuring I rub that magic spot I know will set her off. My blood thrums through my veins with the taste of her on my lips and the feel of her tight, silky sheath around my fingers. The sensations are overwhelming as I plunge my fingers in and out of Harry's heat. Tiny moans and mewls escape her lips while she moves her hips to take me deep. Her heat sears my fingers and I can't wait to feel it around my cock, which is screaming at me to get inside her, but I want her to come again before I do because I'm not sure how long I'll last. I lean in and nip her clit, then suck it into my mouth. The bud pulses against my tongue and her walls tighten around me. Sliding my free hand up her body, beneath her top, I cup her breast and swipe my thumb over her peaked nipple, and she detonates beautifully.

"Finn! Oh my God!" The sentiment bursts from her lips, and pride that I could make her lose control fills me. This time, my mouth is too far away to swallow her cries of pleasure and I hope to God that none of my staff are walking by my office. When her orgasm wanes, I reluctantly remove my fingers and lick them clean, then stand. A wave of dizziness almost knocks me off-balance for a moment, so I close my eyes and grip Harry's hips to steady myself. Too much blood in my cock and not enough in my head on top of standing too fast. Pink cheeks and glassy eyes greet me when I open my eyes again and I can't contain my smirk at seeing what my handiwork does to Harry.

I press my mouth to hers, and she opens eagerly, welcoming me inside. Fishing the condom out of my pocket, I drop my shorts and boxer briefs. Harry tears her lips from mine and takes the condom from my hand and, without hesitation, she opens the packet while glancing down at my dick. Wide eyes meet mine, and she swallows hard. She licks her lips, then pulls out the condom with delicate fingers. I watch her intently, my breath stalling in my lungs. Placing the tip of the condom in her mouth, she purses her lips, slides from the desk, and drops to her knees.

Oh, fuck!

Harry's on her knees in front of me, and I think I know where this is headed. I count backward from ten to stave off my orgasm. There's no way I want to embarrass myself by coming before I even get inside her. She slowly slides her warm mouth down my shaft, rolling the condom on as she goes. Her eyes never leave mine, and the sight stokes the fire inside me into flames that are going to swallow me whole. She uses her fingers to ensure the latex is firmly secured at the base of my dick, and I can't stand it anymore. I grip her beneath her arms and deposit her onto my desk, spreading her legs wide and slamming inside her before I lose my mind. *"Fuck."*

"Holy shit!" Her eyes widen and her mouth drops open in a perfect O. Her cheeks are flushed, and I decide in that instant that I'm going to make it my mission to be inside Harry as often as possible. We fit together perfectly as her body wraps around mine. She locks her feet behind my ass, and her arms wrap around my body to cup my shoulders. I hold still for a few moments, studying her face closely, ensuring I didn't hurt her when I shoved inside her welcoming heat. Sliding my hands from her hips, up her rib cage to her tits, I drag the top of her shirt down and rub my thumbs over her peaked nipples. I need my mouth on them with a desperation I've not felt before, so I tug the cups down, exposing them.

Flawless. Light pink buds, the same shade as her perfect lips.

"Look at these pretty nipples, waiting for my mouth."

Lowering my head, I take one perfect breast into my mouth, sucking hard on the plump flesh and swirling my tongue around the peak. The vibration of Harry's moan tickles my lips, and she slides her fingers through my hair, gripping it tight to hold me in place. She needn't worry. I'd stay here sucking on her pretty nipples all night if she'd let me. Her sighs and whimpers tell me she likes what I'm doing, so I switch to her other breast and then move my hips. Meeting me thrust for thrust, she tightly grips my hair with one hand and digs her short fingernails into my shoulder with the other. I love that I'll have her marks on me when we're done. It'll be the perfect reminder that this happened, and it wasn't a figment of my imagination.

Kissing and sucking my way up to her mouth, I grasp Harry's hips and tug her to the edge of the desk so I can hammer into her. I increase my thrusts like an animal, slamming into her pussy over and over again. I want her to still feel me when she lays down to sleep tonight and when she wakes in the morning. I want her to feel me for days. I want her to lust after my cock the way I've lusted after her since I first laid eyes on her. I want her so desperate she can't stay away, that she'll have no choice but to seek me out and ride my cock every chance she gets.

Harry raises her feet, resting her heels on the edge of my desk, opening herself wider for me. My hips have a mind of their own, snapping forward relentlessly, filling her and retreating, over and over. Her moans and breathy sighs urge me on. Silky walls tighten around my cock and telltale tingles make their way down my spine.

I'm so damn close. "Look at how beautifully your pussy takes my cock."

She drops her eyes to where we are joined and moans.

I move my hand slightly and tease her clit with the pad of

my thumb. Harry's mouth drops open and her breaths fan across the side of my face. Pressing her sensitive bud firmly, I take her mouth in a hard kiss and she breaks apart beneath me. Gray fills the edge of my vision and my balls draw up tight, then my release bursts out of me and into the condom. Pulse after hot pulse. It seems as though it's never going to end, and I throw my head back with a long groan.

Harry licks her way from the base of my throat up to my jawline, so I drop my head and capture her mouth. Our tongues fight for dominance, and I love that she's not shy. That she brings her fire. Holding my slowly softening cock inside Harry's velvet heat, I slide my hand around to the back of her head, grip the silky strands at the base and direct her head exactly where I want it. I kiss her deep, trying to reach down to her soul.

I want her to remember this.

I want my taste seared into her flesh.

I want her to ache for me.

"Finn." The door handle rattles and we pull apart abruptly. Thank fuck I locked the door. Knocking sounds, and I trace my eyes over Harry's face. She's as startled as I am. I disengage, quickly removing the condom and pulling up my boxer briefs and shorts.

Harry drops to her feet, grabbing her panties. "Who's that?" she whispers as she quickly redresses.

"My day bar manager, Blaze." I readjust Harry's top. "He should have left by now. Something must be up." I scan my eyes over Harry to make sure she's presentable as she brushes her fingers through her messy curls. As much as we've tried to put ourselves back together, Blaze is going to take one look at us and know exactly what we've been doing in here. "I need to see what he wants. You okay?" I take a step closer to the door as Harry nods.

Cracking the door, I use my body to block the entrance,

but my footing is unstable and Blaze pushes through. Harry takes a startled step back as she settles her purse across her body. Blaze's eyes dart around my office and scan her from head to toe, then return to me. A snarky smirk lifts his lips, and I don't like the look in his eyes. I take a step closer to Harry, putting my body in front of hers and blocking her from Blaze's roving gaze. "Why are you still here? Is there something you needed?"

"I needed to talk to you about something." His answer is vague, and it pisses me off. I was having a moment with Harry, and he interrupted it for *something*.

"Can't it wait 'til tomorrow? I need to get to soccer."

Harry touches my back, searing my flesh. "I should go. You have things to do and I need to get home." She steps around both of us and escapes out the door before I can say anything, taking my after-sex buzz with her.

Blaze follows her out with his eyes, then sniffs the air and turns to me. "You fucked her in your office?" He raises his eyebrows and rests his hands on his hips, waiting for an answer —one he won't be getting. And while he may appear casual, I know him and I can read the tension bunched tight in his body.

I move behind my desk, ignoring his question. "What did you need?"

"We're not gonna talk about the boss fucking some random in the office. I thought messing around with the patrons was against the rules. Isn't that why you put me on a warning?" He leans over my desk, trying to intimidate me.

"Get to the point. I have somewhere I need to be." I grab my keys and bend down to collect my bag.

"Considering what I just walked in on, I wanna know when the warning on my file gets cleared."

Stepping from behind my desk, I walk past him. "I don't know what you *think* you walked in on, but the two events are completely unrelated. The warning stays until I'm certain I can trust you to treat our patrons with respect."

"Is that what you were doing?" he snarks behind me.

I spin on my heel and move forward, anger bubbling to the surface. "You need to remember whom you're speaking to, Blaze. I'm not one of the guys, and the fact you're speaking to me like this shows you still haven't found the respect I expect you to have." I head back to the door and open it. "Go home, Blaze. I'll see you tomorrow."

He huffs as he walks past me. I can't help but feel that Blaze's time working at *Brady's* is coming to an end, which sucks because he's a decent manager, and bar managers are difficult to find.

I spin in my chair and roll closer to my desk, dragging my laptop forward as I do. I pause as my gaze catches on the opposite side of the desk where I took Harry earlier. My lips pull up as I remember her breaking apart around me beautifully. As much as I wanted to have her from the moment I laid eyes on her, I never imagined it would happen, and in my office, no less. I shake my head, drawing my eyebrows tight. She deserves more than a quick fuck on an office desk. I should go over there tomorrow and apologize for my behavior. It was disrespectful.

Though I wouldn't mind being disrespectful again.

I sigh heavily and tear my eyes away from *the spot*, opening my laptop. I scan the forty-two emails waiting for me. Huh? What's this? An email from Harry. A level of excitement makes its way through my body, and I quickly click on it.

From: Harry Dubois <harry@harryshouse.com>

To: Mr. Brady <manager@bradyspub.com>

Dear Mr. Brady

We're back to being formal, I see.

Earlier this evening, I came to speak with you regarding a matter involving your business. However, we became sidetracked by another matter, and I didn't get the opportunity to speak with you about it.

A smirk touches my lips, and I raise my eyes to my closed office door. Hell yeah, we got sidetracked.

Each afternoon between 4 and 5 p.m. I take delivery of fresh ingredients for my café. My suppliers normally park behind my café for ease of delivery; however, access has been blocked by a truck parked in the alleyway between your business and mine for the last ten days.

At first, I thought it was a one-off thing, but after three days, I began to get annoyed. Now, ten days on, it seems as though the owner of the vehicle has developed a habit. It means my suppliers have to park down the street and we have to carry the stock over a longer distance. A job that took fifteen minutes at most now takes up to forty minutes, depending on how far away they need to park.

You can imagine the inconvenience this causes my suppliers and me. I began taking photographs after the third day (please see attached).

I click on the first attachment and anger burns swiftly. What the fuck is going on? Blaze doesn't need to park his truck in the alleyway, so why the sudden need to do it now? It's like he's trying to cause issues between us and the neighbors.

I kindly ask that you speak with the individual responsible. The alleyway is meant to be kept clear, so this is a breach of the council ordinance.

I hit reply.

I'll speak with my employee first thing in the morning. I apologize for the inconvenience caused and assure you this matter will be dealt with swiftly.
When can I see you again?

Now I have to give Blaze a second warning. It's almost like he's trying to lose this job.

Callahan steps into my office, his face set in stern lines. "Shit's still going missing, so I've set up a discreet camera in the storeroom."

"How discreet?"

"Nobody will know it's there unless they know to look for a camera in the first place. And even then, it'll be tough to find."

"Good. Thanks. Hopefully, we can get to the bottom of the issue."

"No problem. It's pissing me off that someone's taking advantage of their position and your trust. When we find out who it is, I'll wring their damn neck myself." I have a sneaking suspicion I already know who it is, but this will give me the evidence we'll need to take action. "I'm off for the night. Need anything else before I go?"

"Nah. Go home." He turns to leave. "And thanks again, Cal."

"No problem."

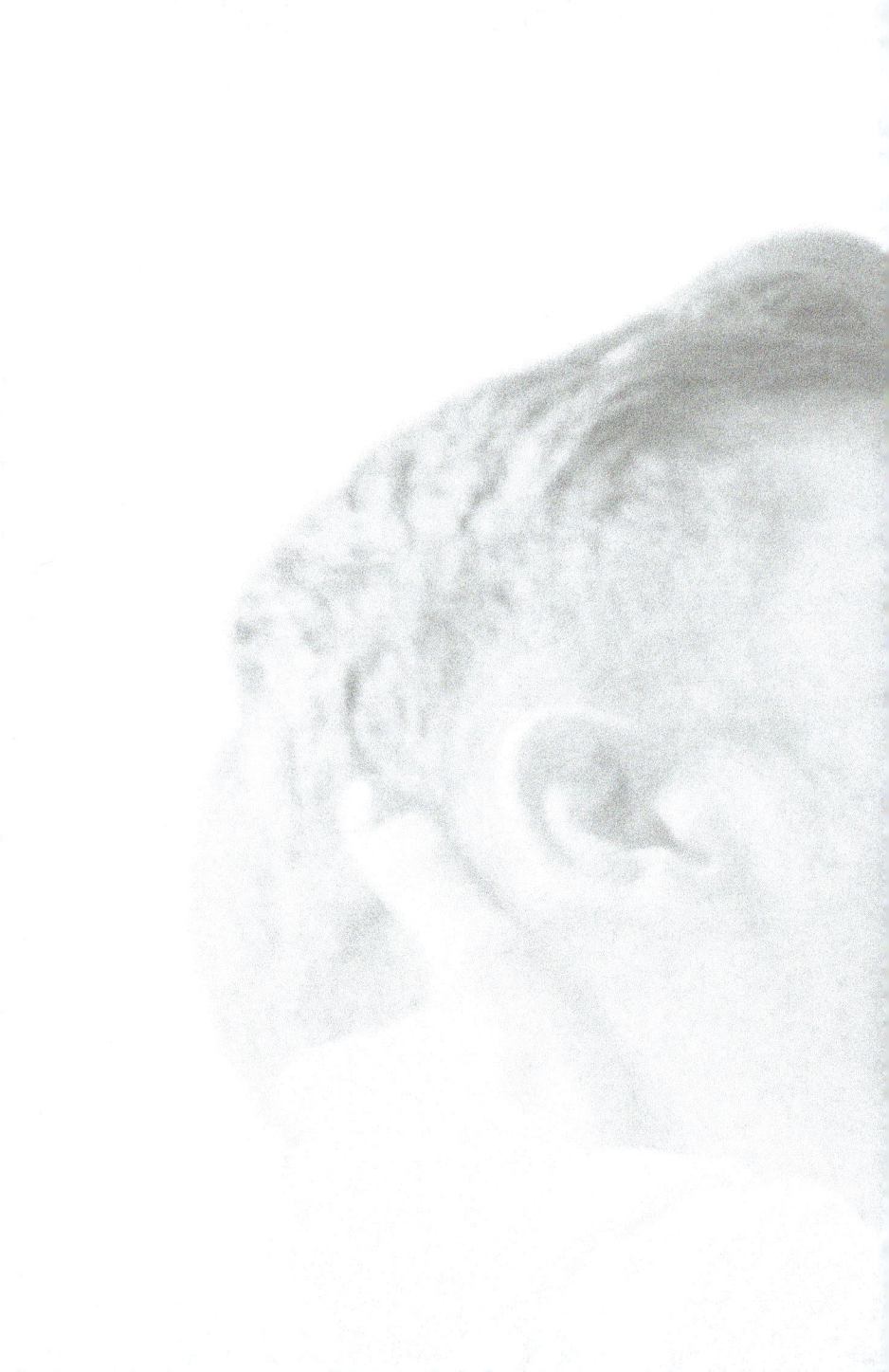

CHAPTER 15

—harriet—

IT'S WEDNESDAY. ONE OF MY FAVORITE DAYS OF THE WEEK. I always look forward to spending my afternoon with Beverley and Frank.

"What are you smiling about?" Matthew asks as he wipes the tables and stacks the chairs.

"It's Wednesday."

A crease forms between his brows. "Oh-kay," he responds slowly.

"On Wednesdays, I visit my friends, Beverley and Frank. They're so much fun to spend time with."

He nods. "Oh, okay. Sounds cool."

"Did she tell you that Beverley and Frank live in a nursing home?" Judy breezes through with the broom while I scrub the display fridge.

Matthew's head snaps around to me. "You hang out with old people, and you think it's fun? You need to get out more, Harry." He chuckles.

My eyebrows shoot up at his jesting. He's been with us for four weeks and slowly but surely he's grown more comfortable with us, joining in with jokes and conversations. He settled in quickly and is a fast learner. Quentin's impressed with his work in the kitchen. Even though I didn't initially employ him for food preparation, he's picked up the techniques like he was born to be a pastry chef.

"Ha ha." I poke my tongue at him like the mature adult I am.

We finish cleaning, then Matthew, Judy, and Quentin leave for the day. I step into my office to catch up on my office work while I wait for Stella and Liam with their deliveries, making sure I complete everything so I can leave as soon as I store the produce.

With everything stored ready for the morning, I lock the back door, drop today's treats in my basket, and head off to the nursing home. The wind is intense and my thighs burn against the resistance, but I push on. Thank goodness the temperature has finally dropped from the extreme highs we've been having. My hair blows into my face and my bike wobbles as I push it out of the way so I can see properly.

"*Hoooonk!*" My heart stutters and my balance is precarious as a car speeds past me. Geez. That was a close call. I come to a stop close to the curb to catch my breath and calm my racing heart. Some people are assholes on the road; sometimes I think they don't like sharing the road with cyclists. I take deep breaths until my hands stop shaking, then hit the road again.

When I ride into the parking lot, my shirt is sticking to my body. I hate that. I hate being sweaty. It's a real thing. I know I'm probably a weirdo.

I grab my lock and secure my bike to the fence, then collect the treats out of the basket. My smile is wide as the glass doors slide open and I step into the reception area and walk toward the sign-in desk. Rachel looks up from her computer with a smile, which drops the instant her eyes lock on me. That's weird. My stomach twists. I hope they aren't mad at me for bringing treats for Beverley and Frank.

"Hi, Rachel. I'm here to see Beverley and Frank."

Her gaze skates around the reception area. "Uh, Harry. Could you please wait here a moment?"

I drop my smile and my eyebrows furrow together. "Everything okay?" I ask her retreating back.

She doesn't answer and disappears through a doorway. I sign the visitor's book while I wait for her to come back to unlock the door so I can visit with my friends. A woman I vaguely remember from when Grand-Mère died steps through the doorway, her lips turned down and eyes full of compassion. My heart stutters and a sense of dread climbs up my body from my toes.

She comes around to my side of the reception area and holds out a hand toward the black leather couches on the opposite side of the room. "Harry. Would you mind joining me over here?" She walks in the direction she just pointed, and I follow her on autopilot, the sense of dread growing stronger. I take a seat next to her and swivel my body slightly so we're facing each other. "I'm not sure if you remember me. We met when your grandmother passed." My mouth is too dry to speak, so I nod and she continues. "My name's Andrea and I'm the manager here." I nod again. "We find ourselves in an unusual situation. I contacted Beverley's family this afternoon, and they permitted me to discuss this with you since you visit with Beverley each Wednesday."

I try to swallow past the boulder-sized lump lodged in my throat. My nose is tingling and that telltale sting at the back of my eyes is threatening to burst free. I fidget with the box containing Frank and Beverley's favorite treats. "I-i-is Beverley o-okay?"

Sadness washes over Andrea's face. "I'm so sorry to have to tell you this. But Beverley suffered a massive stroke yesterday morning. She was taken to the hospital—"

I stand on shaky legs. "Which hospital?" I need to visit her.

Andrea stands and places her hand on my shoulder. "I'm sorry, Harriet. Beverley didn't make it. She passed away early this morning." Her words are muffled, and I have to concentrate hard to focus on what she's saying.

The box falls from my hands; the treats spilling onto the pristine carpet, leaving flakes of pastry strewn about. I collapse onto the couch and wrap my arms around my body to hold myself together, but the tears fall as a loud sob escapes.

"I'm so sorry, Harriet. I understand how close you were. The family wanted me to pass on their thanks and appreciation for your regular visits. They were the highlight of her week." She sits beside me and squeezes my arm. "If you would like to attend her funeral, let me know. The family said you would be welcome."

I bury my face in my hands and sob. All the pain of losing Grand-Mère comes back to the surface and threatens to suffocate me. I'm right back to the night when my life changed forever. Andrea wraps her arm around me, pulling me in close to hold my broken pieces together while I fall apart. I try to suck in deep breaths and compose myself, but just as I gather myself, another memory of Beverley assaults me, and I'm back to where I started.

Oh my God. Frank.

I wipe away my tears with the heels of my hands and run my fingers beneath my nose. "How's Frank? He and Beverley were close."

"He hasn't come out of his room and won't speak with anyone. We've been checking on him, but he hasn't moved from his seat by the window in his room."

"C-can I see him?"

Andrea looks away, then back to me. "I'm not sure he'll see you, but you can try. I'll walk you to his room."

"Thank y-you." As we pass the reception desk, Andrea leans over the counter and passes me a wad of tissues. I take them gratefully and wipe my face and blow my nose. Frank's going to know I've been crying. I won't be able to hide it from him. He never misses much. We walk down the long corridors and it seems to take forever. A sob breaks free when we pass Beverley's door. Knowing she's not in there and never will be again rips my heart wide open.

When we reach Frank's door, Andrea knocks softly, then opens it. "Frank. Harriet's here to see you." Frank glances at me, then turns his face back to the window, but there's no mistaking the redness around his eyes and nose. "Is it okay if she comes in for a while?" He simply nods once. Andrea smiles, then touches my arm as she leaves. "Take your time."

I nod. "Th-thank you."

Andrea closes the door quietly behind her, and I stand in silence for a few moments. The two of us have never spent time alone together. We always had Beverley and her wicked sense of humor.

"I loved her, you know," Frank whispers roughly into the silent room. "I didn't think I'd love anyone after my wife died, but I loved Beverley." My feet take on a life of their own and within a few steps, I'm at Frank's side. "It was a different kind of love, but I loved her." He sniffles and I bend down to wrap my arms around him. He doesn't move or reciprocate, but *I* need to hold him in our sadness. "She made this place tolerable."

"I know." I pull back and rest my butt on the edge of Frank's bed. "I can't believe she's gone."

"Me neither."

We sit in silence. Side by side, staring out of Frank's window as late afternoon turns to dusk and dusk turns to night.

The dinner service comes and goes, and neither of us touches the meals left for us. Hours pass and neither of us speaks.

What is there to say?

Voices in the corridor intermittently break the silence in Frank's room. My legs are numb and my mind is blank of everything except the devastating news. I'm sure my face is swollen like a balloon as tears come in waves.

A soft knock sounds on the door, and it opens. "Harriet. I'm so sorry to do this, but it's late. I have to ask you to leave, but you're welcome to return tomorrow."

I move to stand too quickly and lose my balance when I try to put my weight on my feet, which have gone to sleep. I drop my butt back to the bed and try to wriggle my toes to wake them up. "Of course. I understand. I have to work tomorrow, and I have deliveries coming late in the day, so I'm not sure I'll be able to come back tomorrow." The blood rushes back into my feet, and I test to see if I can stand.

Frank glances at me. "Thanks for sitting with me, Harry."

My heart cracks at the raspy nature of his voice. "Any time." I hug him tight and whisper, "I'll be back."

Andrea walks me out and when she notices the parking lot is empty, she turns to me. "How did you get here?"

I point to my bike. "I rode."

"Do you need me to call you an Uber or something?"

"No, thank you. The ride will do me good. Can you please let me know if Frank gets worse?" Andrea nods. "And when Beverley's funeral will be. I'd like to pay my respects."

"Of course."

I climb onto my bike and ride into the night. I don't pay attention to where I'm going. I just pedal, wiping away the tears as they escape down my cheeks. It's so unfair. Beverley had so much life in her. She was always cracking inappropriate jokes and getting up to mischief. I can't believe she's gone. I glance up to the night sky as the wind dries my damp cheeks. "Don't get up to too much mischief together up there."

When I focus back on the road in front of me, the lights from *Brady's Pub* shine brightly in the darkness. I blow out a long breath. I know exactly how I ended up here, even though it wasn't my intention.

I don't want to be on my own.

Not tonight.

And Finn … well … he has this way of making me feel like I could turn to him for comfort and he would hold my broken pieces together for a while. Which is completely unexpected, but exactly what I need. And a drink wouldn't hurt even though I'm not a drinker. Not after watching Dad all my life.

I park and lock my bike behind my café, then head next door. The pub is crazy busy, busier than I expected. Winding my way through the throng of people, it takes a fair amount of maneuvering to get to the bar. There's a woman behind the bar, but it isn't Macy. I find an opening and wedge myself between two burly guys. The male bartender makes his way over to me with a welcoming smile. I glance at his name tag: Gabriel. "What can I get for you?"

Uhhh. I didn't even consider what I would order. I've had limited experience with drinking alcohol, only having tried whiskey and gin twice when I was younger and not being a fan of either. I know that if my dad wasn't drinking rum; he was drinking red wine so neither of those are options for me. "What would you recommend to a person who rarely drinks?" I raise my voice to be heard over the crowd.

He studies me closely and I appreciate that he's taking his time to consider suitable options. "How about a Vodka cran-berry? It's sweet and fruity and you can't taste the alcohol."

I nod. "Sounds good. Thank you."

He tips his head to me and then sets about making my drink. I slide some cash across the bar and take a sip of the sweet concoction. Gabriel watches me closely as I swallow the fruity goodness and then step up on the foot rail so I can thank him. "Thank you. It's delicious. Just what I needed."

"You're welcome. Let me know when you need another." He winks and moves on to serve the next customer.

I spot a stool open up on the other side of the guy next to me, so I quickly grab my drink and perch myself on it. Tracing my fingers down the condensation, my mind wanders back to earlier and the utter devastation on Frank's face. I always knew he had a thing for Beverley, but I had no idea how deep his feelings were.

"Can I get you another?" I look up at the voice. It's the woman this time. Her brows furrow when she sees my face. "Are you okay, hun?"

I shrug. "Not really. And yeah, would you mind?"

"No problem. What are you drinking?"

"Vodka cranberry, please."

She smiles at me and makes my drink. As she slides it across the bar, I hand her my money and ask, "Is it always this busy?"

"When Toby Summer's in the house, it is." She tips her chin toward a set of stairs. "He's playing downstairs and the overflow crowd is up here."

Right. Well, that explains some things. Toby Summer is only one of the most popular musicians around at the moment, and he's a local boy. I had no idea he played at venues like this. I sip my drink slowly, keeping an eye out for Finn, but he's nowhere to be seen.

My bladder screams at me, so I forfeit my stool and make my way down the hallway that leads to Finn's office to visit the bathroom. Then I should head home. I have an early start in the morning, and I'm guessing Finn's probably too busy for me. I'm not sure why I came here; I always manage on my own. When I've finished in the bathroom, a familiar-looking man is leaning against the wall opposite with his arms crossed in front of his thick body. He's a big guy, probably bigger than Quentin.

Where do I know him from?

He glances up and a sly smirk lifts one side of his lips and a predatory gleam shines in his eyes. I quickly drop my gaze to the floor and scurry down the hallway, only to have a big hand wrap around my bicep and pull me to a stop. My heart hammers in my chest and my skin becomes too tight.

"What's the rush, beautiful?"

I struggle to come up with a reason that doesn't let him know I'm here on my own. Even though I'm sure Finn's here somewhere, he can't help me right now. "Uh, my friends are waiting to go downstairs to watch Toby Summer."

"Is that right? I didn't notice any friends when you were sitting at the bar." He spins me around and pins me against the wall with his bulky body.

Blood pounds in my ears and sweat coats my spine. *Shit.*

"I'm meeting them downstairs."

His grin turns sinister. "Don't lie to me, beautiful." He runs his nose up my neck, following my jawline to my ear. His disgusting breath coats my face as he moves. I pull my head as far back as possible, but I can only go so far with the wall behind me. "How about letting me sample the goods you gave up so easily for the boss?"

Now I recognize him. He's Finn's day bar manager.

He licks his way from my ear, along my jawline to my other ear, pushing his disgusting cock into my stomach. I close my eyes tight. Maybe if I can't see him, he'll disappear. His putrid breath surrounds me and I try to hold my breath as I push him with all my strength.

Suddenly, his weight is gone.

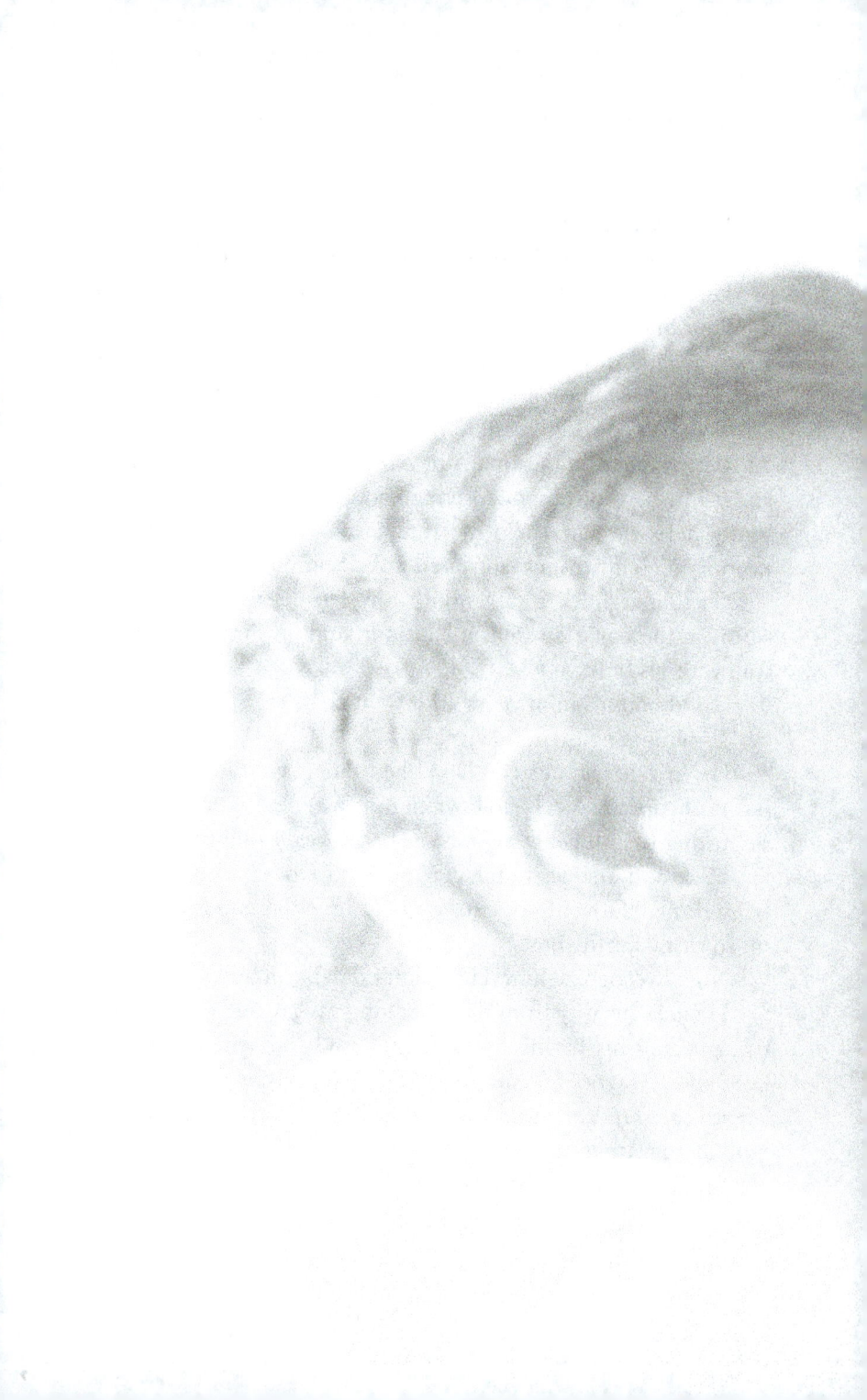

CHAPTER 16

—finn—

THE MINUTE I STEP THROUGH THE DOORS TO THE PUB, MACY calls out, "Phone for you!"

It's still early enough that the main bar is only at one-third capacity. I stride across the room and grab the phone. "Finn Brady. How can I help you?"

"Finn. It's Toby Summer."

"Toby. Good to hear from you, man. It's been a while since I've seen you."

His sigh sounds across the phone. "Yeah. I've been busy writing and getting married." He chuckles. "I was hoping I could come down and test out some of my new stuff."

"Absolutely, man. Any time you wanna come down, just come. Do you want me to get the word out or do you want to just show up and play to whoever's here?"

Silence greets me. "Let's do a spontaneous show."

"No problem. When are you thinking?"

"How about tonight?"

"Sure. The band we had booked for tonight canceled yesterday because their lead singer has tonsillitis."

"That works. See you at eight."

"See you then."

I hang up the phone and turn to Macy, who's waiting with raised brows. "Toby Summer's coming down to play tonight."

Her cheeks flush pink, and she plays with her hair. "I'd better increase my cocktail prep. We're about to be overrun by a bunch of horny women."

I laugh. "I guess once word gets out, but he doesn't want us to let anyone know he's coming down." We get busy prepping for cocktails because Macy's right. Even though Toby wants it to be spontaneous, it won't take long for word to spread on social media, and we'll end up with hordes of women. Even when he drops into the pub for a drink with his friend and bodyguard, Shane, the number of women in the pub doubles rapidly. It's going to be more out of control if he's playing.

I call Nix to see if he's able to provide additional security for tonight. Thankfully, he's able to help with a few of his guys at short notice. Blaze agrees to stay on for the night shift to help with the anticipated crowd.

As expected, the pub is packed, and even though Toby brought his wife with him it hasn't reduced the number of women pouring into the pub.

"Finn, can you grab more Vodka from upstairs?" Macy shouts in my ear over the noise.

I nod and head upstairs to the storeroom. As I wander down the back hallway, I spot Blaze towering over a woman. His posture is menacing, and I don't like it.

Not on my premises. Not on my time. Not ever.

He's already had one warning about this type of behavior. Whoever's trapped against the wall must give him a shove, because his body moves an inch, revealing warm brown curls. Curls I've had sliding between my fingers.

I take off from my spot and use my momentum to knock Blaze out of the way. He stumbles slightly, so I take advantage of him being off balance and aim my fist at his jaw. My knuckles connect with what feels like stone. *Fuck! That hurt.* "Get the fuck off my premises and don't come back. You're fired," I shout. I can't remember the last time I felt so damn pissed.

He grips his jaw and narrows his eyes at me. "What the fuck, man?"

I move between him and Harry, protecting her with my body. "You heard me. Get your shit out of the office and get out."

"You can't fucking fire me. You need me."

"I can and I don't." My voice is full of steel. "You're nothing but trouble. You've already had a warning about this shit."

He studies me for a moment and then his eyes flick to Harry, whose hands are now gripping each side of my shirt. "Fuck you." He spins on his heel and sends me the bird over his shoulder. "This pub is a shit place to work anyway."

Once he's out of sight, I take a calming breath and run my hand through my hair. Fuck. That was intense. Once I feel more in control, I turn to face Harry. Tracing my gaze over her from head to toe, her puffy eyes and red nose tell me she's been crying. "Are you okay?"

"I-I just came in for a drink because I didn't want to go home after finding out my friend d-di-died. I didn't want to be a-alone," she sobs. Her tears come in full force. *Did she say her friend died? Oh shit.*

I wrap my arm around her and pull her in tight to my body, then cup the back of her head and press her in close to lay a kiss on top of her head. Her arms tangle around me and she buries her face in my chest as she cries for her loss. I would guess that the shock of what just happened wouldn't be helping. We stand, locked together in the busy hallway close to the bathrooms.

Blaze storms out of my office carrying a box, shooting me the filthiest look known to man. I'm not sure how I'm still standing in one piece. Once he clears the hallway, I gently walk backward—without releasing Harry—into my office and close the door. The silence inside is a stark contrast to the noisy pub and now that I'm alone with Harry in here, I'm not sure what to do. Whenever I'm with her, I want to do filthy things to her, but those thoughts are the furthest from my mind right now. I want to comfort her and take away her pain. I want to draw it out of her and eliminate her sadness. I want to see sparks flying from her eyes, not tears falling from them. My heart constricts as I guide her to my couch and take a seat, situating Harry across my lap. She still has her face buried in my chest, but her sobs have subsided. We sit in the quiet as I rub her back with gentle strokes and allow her the time she needs.

My office door bursts open. Cal stands in the opening, and the noise of the pub breaks the silence like a gunshot. Harry jumps at the sudden intrusion but buries herself further into me, which encourages me to tighten my hold on her. "Wha—" His words die on his tongue as his eyes land on Harry in my lap.

It's then I remember what I was supposed to be doing before I found Blaze standing over Harry. "Cal. Can you take more Vodka down to Macy, please?"

"Sure. We need to talk when you're free." He closes the door and my office falls silent again.

Harry pulls back from my hold, and I loosen my grip. "I sh-should go. You're busy and you don't need me taking up your time."

She pushes to stand but I tighten my hold again. "You're not going anywhere. You'll stay here for as long as you need."

"But—" I press my finger over her lips to stop her.

"No buts."

Harry sinks back into my body, and a sense of calm I'm not familiar with settles over me. I want to provide her with a safe place to fall apart. It feels as important as breathing. "You didn't have to fire your employee on my behalf," Harry whispers into my shirt.

I sure as fuck did. I don't want anyone on my payroll who thinks it's okay to intimidate women. And it's not only because it was Harry. If I caught him doing that to any woman again after his first warning, I would have fired his ass on the spot. He's been causing trouble around here for a while now. "Don't worry about Blaze. He needed to go. I don't want people like him on my staff. His behavior was unacceptable. If you want to press charges, you can. I have surveillance along that hallway. It would have caught everything on tape."

She shakes her head. "I'm not sure he did enough to warrant charges. He was intimidating and I'm sure if you hadn't come along when you did, things might have ended up worse, but that didn't happen … thanks to you."

I want to push it further because this isn't the first time Blaze has done something similar, but I don't think now is the time to do it. She's just lost her friend, so I'll let it go for now.

She sighs and sinks farther into me. And I like it. I want her wrapped in my arms for always. I want her pain, her sadness, her fire, her smile. I want everything with her. Suddenly, all I see is a future laid out in front of me, playing like a movie, and she's front and center in every scene. Her breathing slows and deepens, and I think she's fallen asleep. I stroke her hair gently away from her face, tracing my fingers along her jaw and down to her chin. I'm dying to tilt her face up to mine so I can kiss her, but she's distraught and I'm not one to take advantage. I kiss the top of her head and as I'm getting comfortable for a long night ahead; she stirs and tilts her face up to mine. Her sad eyes trace over every part of my face, pausing on my lips. Desire replaces the sadness and her delicate tongue swipes across her bottom lip, making it shine.

"Please kiss me," she murmurs and I give up the fight to hold myself back.

Closing the distance, I gently press my lips to hers, tasting her tears, the sweetness of cranberry, and Harry. I want to devour her, but I move slowly, patiently. She sighs into my mouth, and I swallow it greedily, hungry for more. Opening my mouth, Harry mirrors the action and our tongues taste, tease, and tangle for what seems like an eternity. I slide my hand up her back until I reach her nape, then tighten my grip around the strands of her silky curls as Harry wraps her delicate fingers in my shirt, pulling me in tight against her body. Our kiss deepens and becomes more urgent. Harry twists her body, so she's straddling my lap and grinds down on my aching cock.

God, I want to be inside her.

She shifts her hips, changing her angle, and grinds down again. It feels so fucking good that I can't contain my groan, which comes from deep inside me. I drop my hands to her hips and guide her movements, ensuring she gets the friction she's seeking. "Do you need to come, Firecracker?" Her eyes snap open, revealing dilated pupils to the point there is only a thin ring of green surrounding them and she nods. "Tell me."

Her gaze darts back and forward between my eyes and she swallows. I urge her to give me the words I need with my eyes and study her closely while she decides whether she's going to give me what I want. "Please make me come, Finn. Make me forget for a little while."

I slam my mouth onto hers, pushing my tongue between her swollen lips, and tightening my grip on her hips. Small grunts leave my lips every time her heat makes contact with my cock and mix with her whimpers, which are increasing in pitch as she climbs closer to her peak. I need to concentrate hard to make sure I don't come in my boxers like a seventeen-year-old kid on his first fucking date. I can't remember the last time I was dry-humped. Harry presses her lips against mine softly, her warm breath filling the minuscule space between us. "Harder," she whispers.

"Take what you need," I grunt, sliding my hands up to her gorgeous breasts, allowing Harry to set the pace she needs. Pushing my hips up to match her movements, I cup the mounds and pinch her nipples through the fabric of her bra, while running my lips along her collarbone and up her throat, licking the pulse point at the base on the way.

Her panting increases as her movements become jerky. Her warm breath coats my face as I watch her come undone in my lap, moaning her release into my quiet office. I press her hips down, holding her tight to my body to stave off my orgasm. Harry drops her forehead to my shoulder and we sit in silence while she catches her breath. I stroke my hands up and down her back, feeling her body move with each inhale and exhale. Her movements change, becoming jerky. Her forehead still rests on my shoulder, so I can't see her face, but I hope to hell she isn't crying again. I don't think my heart can take any more.

"Are you okay?" My breath stutters in my chest at the tears painting her cheeks. "What's wrong?"

"I shouldn't have done that. I don't know what came over me." She drops her eyes to my chest and her cheeks flush pink.

"You've had a terrible day, Harry." I tap her gorgeous ass. "I'm glad I could make you feel better, if even for a moment. C'mon, I'm taking you home."

A small crease forms between her brows. "What about you?"

"What about me?"

"Did you ... uh ... I mean, can I ... uh ... help you out?" She looks pointedly at my dick.

I take a moment to work out what she's asking and even though I'm still rock hard, I'd rather take my time tonight and give Harry the loving she deserves, the loving she *needs* after losing her friend. "I'm good for now." I press a kiss on her forehead and then help her stand. Taking her hand in mine, I lead her to the door. I probably should stay given how busy it is and being a man down already, but I can't bring myself to do it. Not tonight.

I pull Harry down the hallway to the back entrance and usher her outside into the cool night air, then lead her to my car. I shoot a quick message to Callahan to let him know I've left, and that I'll need to see him in the morning. Harry tugs on my hand, pulling me to a stop. "I have my bike. I can ride home."

"You're not riding your bike at this time of night, and if you think I'm letting you go home by yourself, you're sorely mistaken." I hope I'm conveying how much her words displease me.

That fire that I love so much comes blazing to life. "I'm more than capable of looking after myself, thank you very much. I've been doing it for a long time. I ride my bike everywhere unless the weather's shitty"—she holds her hands away from her body—"and I've survived just fine." I'm pretty sure sparks just flew from her eyes, and I grin as I tug her back into me.

I wrap my arms around her, trapping her arms by her side. She doesn't try to escape, but she holds herself stiffly in my embrace. "I know you're more than capable, but I *want* to look after you tonight." I smooth her hair away from her face and press my lips to her forehead. "You've had a shitty day, and I want to hold you. Let me look after you," I whisper and her body softens as she melts into me.

"Okay," she murmurs.

We lock her bike inside her café and make our way to my place. The ride is silent, with Harry keeping her gaze out the passenger window. I reach across and take her hand, placing it on my thigh and holding it there, allowing her to have her quiet moment. I'm certain she must be feeling pretty low after losing her friend.

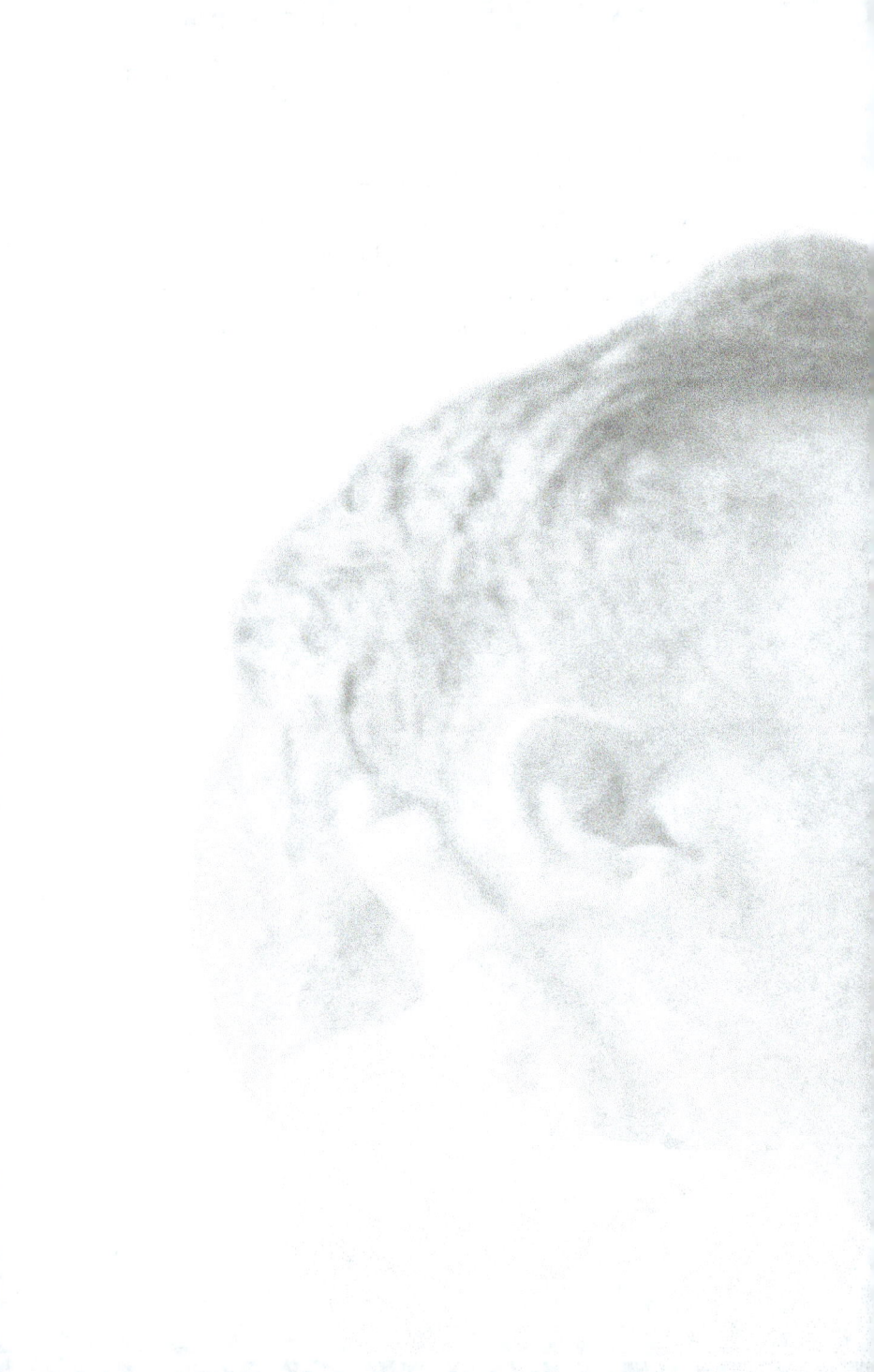

CHAPTER 17
—harriet—

I HADN'T GIVEN MUCH THOUGHT TO WHERE FINN LIVED, BUT IF I had, I don't think I would have pictured him living in a tidy home in the suburbs close to the city center. Maybe an apartment, but not a house. A house suggests Finn wants to get married and have a family one day. As soon as the thought enters my mind, I can't stop the flood of images of me and Finn living here. Him playing in the yard with our three young boys, while I make delicious pastries in the kitchen. Geez, nothing like getting ahead of myself. The guy's given me a couple of orgasms, and I'm already planning out our entire future. But really, he's given me more than a couple of orgasms. He's made me feel safe and cherished. *Important even.*

"It's not much, but it's home. Make yourself comfortable and I'll get us a drink." He kisses my temple and then nudges me toward his living room. The furnishings are sparse, and there aren't any homely touches; I would even go so far as to say that a woman has never lived here. Finn steps into the room with two glasses, passing one to me.

I take a tentative sip, surprised to find it's the same as I was drinking at his pub earlier. My eyes snap across to Finn. "How did you know?"

He gives me that cocky smirk, the one I wanted to slap off his face but now find strangely endearing. "I tasted it on you." Of course he could. I'm sure he's an expert when it comes to alcohol, though I sense he doesn't partake regularly—another thing I find surprising.

"What are you having?"

"Whiskey." He holds his glass toward me. "Would you like a taste?"

I *would* like a taste, but not from his glass. I lean forward and swipe my tongue across the seam of his lips and he opens to allow me entry. As I press my lips to his, I slip my tongue inside his mouth and taste the whiskey. I've never cared for whiskey, but on Finn's tongue, it could easily become an addiction. His free hand finds the back of my head and he moans into my mouth as I kiss him with abandon. I want to pick up where we left off in his office. As great as the orgasm was, I want ... no ... *need* Finn inside me. He tears his lips away and presses his forehead to mine.

"I'm trying to be a gentleman here, Harry." He clenches his jaw. "But you make it damn hard."

My heart pounds a fast rhythm behind my ribs at the blatant need on his too-handsome face. "Take me to bed then." He skates his eyes around my face, then finishes the rest of his drink, so I do the same. He takes my empty glass and places it on the coffee table, then stands and hauls me to my feet. Taking my hand in his, he drags me through the rest of his darkened home toward his bedroom.

"I'll give you a tour tomorrow," he murmurs as he picks me up and unceremoniously tosses me into the middle of his bed. I giggle as I bounce, then Finn lands on top of me. His weight is delicious as he presses me into the mattress; the heat of his body seeping through our clothes and heating my flesh. We quickly become a writhing tangle of hands and touches, kisses, and bites.

"I need you. I need your skin against mine." In the darkness, I find the bottom of his shirt and glide my hands beneath the cotton fabric, making contact with the smooth expanse of his muscular back. At my touch, he moans into my mouth and grinds his hard length against me. "Help me forget about today," I whisper against his lips.

He nods once and climbs off me, pulling me to my feet. His shadowy form moves away from me, and I hear the click of a switch, then soft light bathes his bedroom. He steps back in front of me and slips his hands beneath my sweater, slipping it from my shoulders and dragging it down my arms. "I can make you forget. I can also be a good listener when you're ready to talk about it."

I can't believe I ever thought Finn was anything other than the kind man he's shown himself to be. Layer by layer, he methodically removes every stitch of fabric from my body, kissing and caressing every inch of me as it becomes free from constraints—his hands and mouth feel incredible against my heated skin. My heart pounds a heavy beat for what's about to happen. Once I'm completely bare, he begins removing his clothes, but I tenderly push his hands out of the way. "Let me do it."

He nods stiffly. I do as he did, removing every article of clothing, trailing my hands and lips over his masculine frame as each inch of skin is revealed. He watches me intently as I finally remove his navy boxer briefs, capturing his heavy length in my hand. Squeezing firmly, I lick my lips and lower myself to my knees, but before they can hit the floor, his hands grip me beneath my arms. Shaking his head, he pulls me up. "Another time. Right now I need your pussy around my cock."

Moisture pools at the apex of my thighs, and I press them together to stem my arousal. Finn pushes my thighs apart and swipes his fingers through my slit, groaning at the slickness he finds before bringing them to his lips and tasting my essence. I wrap my hand firmly around his shaft and swipe my thumb across the head, then mimic him, dragging my thumb down my tongue, tasting his salty precum. Watching each other is our undoing, and our mouths slam together in a fierce kiss as our hands explore each other's bodies. The dips and valleys, and smooth skin over taut muscle. The smattering of blond hair across his tanned chest and that sexy trail that leads down to an impressive dick.

God, I need him inside me with a desperation I *know* I've never experienced before—I may die if he doesn't get inside me in the next ten seconds. I don't even care that this is so completely uncharacteristic of me. I need him. *Now!* I tear my mouth from his. "I need you inside me now."

One side of his mouth tips up and his pupils expand to swallow the cobalt of his eyes. He pushes me back, and I land sprawled out on his bed. "Show me how wet you are." I spread my legs open and cup one of my breasts. He groans and reaches into his bedside drawer while stroking his erection. He tears his hand away from his dick and frantically digs around the drawer. "*Fuck.*" He turns his head to me, his eyes full of apology. "I don't have any condoms here. This was unexpected. I didn't bring you back here to have sex. I wanted to take care of you. I hope you know that."

My body softens and my desperation subsides slightly— without him having said it, I knew that was his intention. In this moment, the sexy man standing before me digs himself even deeper into my heart. It's been a slow and gradual fall, but I've fallen in love with him. I reach out for him and he slides the palm of his large hand across mine, sending sparks shooting up my arm and through my body. "I know. I just wanted to forget about the hurt for a little while."

He drops his forehead to mine, our eyes catching and locking. "I can do other things to help you forget." He kisses my shoulder and licks his way down to my breast.

"We can do more than that if you trust me. I'm clean and I'm on the pill to regulate my periods."

His eyes widen. "You trust me that much?"

"Yeah," I say the single word with the utmost certainty. I know we started on the wrong foot, but everything he's shown me since then says he's a man with a strong moral compass.

"I'm clean too." He takes my mouth in a hard kiss, laying me down and spreading out on top of me. His weight is delicious as he grinds down on me, pressing me into the mattress. I wrap my arms around his neck and my legs around his slim hips, drawing him tight to me as we devour each other.

The heat between us is incredible, and it doesn't take long before we're both grinding and exploring each other's bodies with our hands and mouths. He plucks and nips at my breasts, bringing my aching nipples to hard peaks before soothing them with gentle licks and kisses.

An inferno builds inside me, and I lift my hips, seeking the head of his cock. He realizes what I want and draws back slightly. "Are you ready for me, Firecracker?"

"Please," I moan. Lifting my head from the pillow to chase his lips, he dips down, licking across the swollen flesh as he sheaths himself inside me inch by magnificent inch. We both moan in pleasure, and I squeeze my muscles around his cock.

"Ah, fuck. Do that again." I do as he asks and as I squeeze, he moves. The sensation of his smooth cock moving against my tight muscles is better than anything I've ever felt. I press my head into the pillow and tighten my hold around his hips and squeeze him again. "Fuck. If you keep doing that, this is going to be over before we get started." The chuckle that was bubbling up dies in my throat as he slides out and pushes back in … *hard*.

"Oh my God. Do that again." He does as I ask over and

over again. The force of his powerful thrusts shunts me up the bed until the top of my head bangs against the headboard each time he pushes inside, but I'm too lost in the sensations to care. Finn doesn't miss it and cups the top of my head as he changes the angle of his hips slightly. Suddenly, he's hitting a whole different part of me that coils my muscles tight.

I seek his lips and glide my tongue against his until I break apart. Every molecule of my body shatters apart and I pull away to cry out.

"That's it, Harry. You're so fucking beautiful when you come." He kisses me roughly and continues to pump his hips as I ride out my release. Digging my fingernails into his tight backside, he groans into my mouth, then buries himself deep. As I squeeze my core, I feel his cock pulse and he fills me with his cum. His face is etched in what looks like pain as he throws his head back in ecstasy, the muscles in his neck tight, the veins bulging. I raise my head and lick my way down his throat to where his pulse point is hammering a heavy staccato, tasting the saltiness of his skin.

Our bodies are slick with sweat and as he lowers himself against me, the heavy thumping of his heart matches mine. I glide my hands up and down the smooth skin of his back, trailing my short fingernails along his spine in soothing strokes. He captures my mouth again, this time in a slow, languid, sexy kiss while his hands cup my head tenderly and his hips slowly move again. This time, our movements are slow, measured, stoking the flames carefully back to life. Gone is our desperation for release. In its place is something deeper. Something more meaningful. *More intimate.*

Our mouths remain fused as our hips move in sync, my body tightening again, ready for release. Finn incrementally increases his movements, grinding against my sensitive bud each time he bottoms out, taking me closer to the brink. I tighten my legs around his hips to the point I'm surprised he's able to move at all. As my muscles tighten from my toes to the top of my head, I lose myself in my orgasm, with Finn following close behind.

He carefully rolls to the side, taking me with him, and brushes my sweaty curls away from my face. Kissing the tip of my nose, then my forehead, he tugs me in tight to his body, his hand running the length of my spine to cup my ass and raise my leg to rest on top of his.

I could stay wrapped up in him forever.

Finn doesn't seem to be in a hurry to disengage, and I'm happy to stay exactly where I am. His warm hand glides up and down my back in soothing strokes as our heart rates and breathing return to normal.

With his lips a mere breath from mine, Finn whispers, "How are you feeling?"

I skim my eyes over his face, noting the worry in his eyes. "I lost a good friend today. And it may sound weird because she was over ninety, but she was probably one of my best friends." He lovingly strokes my hair back from my face. "Losing her brought back painful memories of losing my grand-mère." That stupid lump has found its way back into my throat and my eyes sting. I blink to stem the tears I know are waiting to fall, but as Finn looks at me with compassion, the dam breaks and they trail their way down the side of my face, into my hair, and across the bridge of my nose.

Finn wipes them away with a delicate swipe of his thumb. "I'm so sorry, Firecracker." He holds me tighter to his warm body and I relish in the feel of being pressed against him. "If there's anything I can do, please let me help."

I nod against his soft lips as he presses them to my forehead. "Thank you. You've already helped so much." We lay quietly in each other's arms for a long time. Until our breathing slows and sleep claims us.

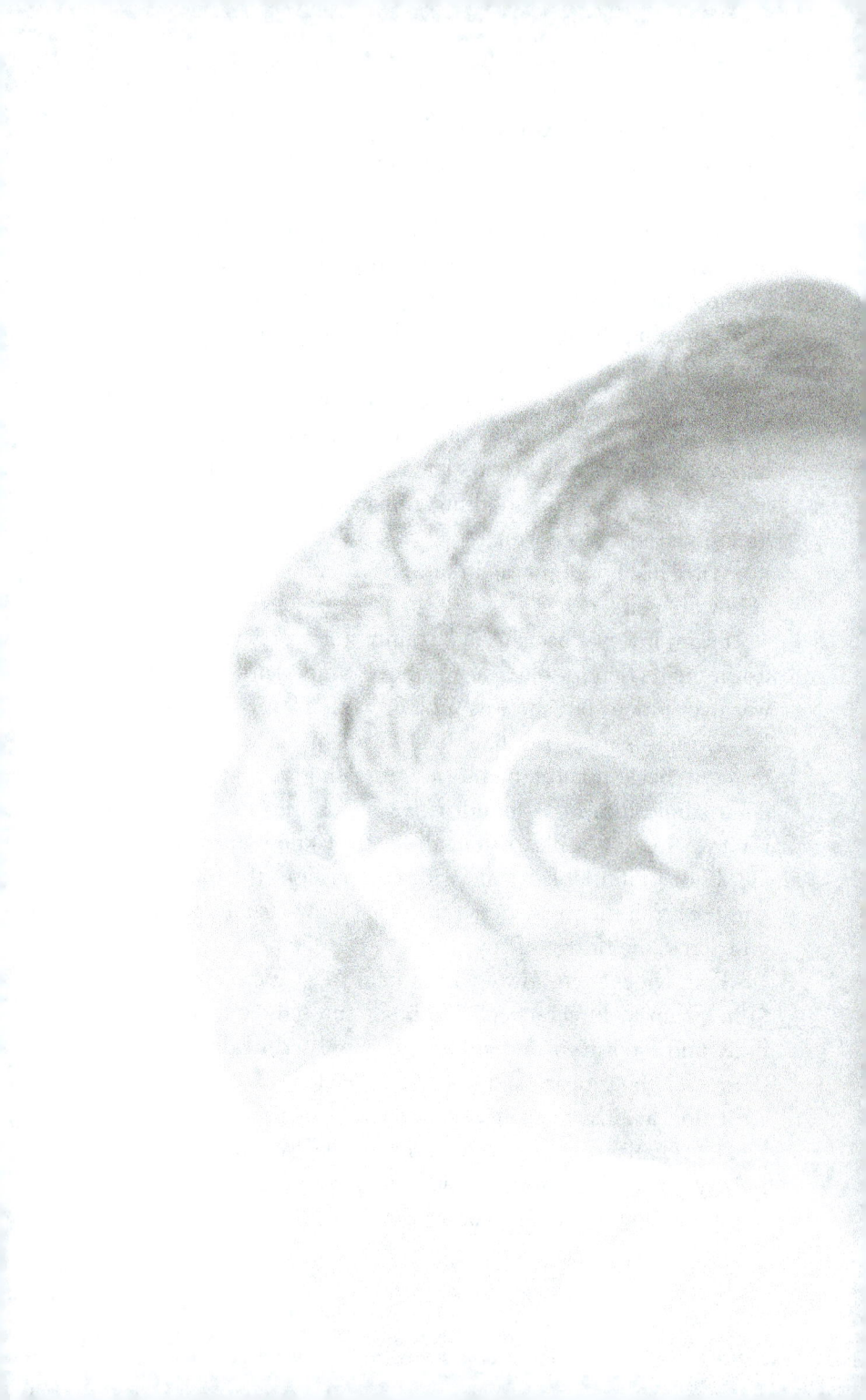

CHAPTER 18

—finn—

Bzzzzz. Bzzzzz.

What the fuck is that?

I peel my eyes open to find my bedroom still dark. Harry stirs on my chest and I tighten my hold on her, drawing in a deep breath of her sweet scent. My heart broke for her last night when she told me about Beverley's passing and the connection to her grandmother.

She hums against my chest. "I need to get up." Raising her head, she looks at me. "Sorry I woke you. I need to get ready for work."

I groan internally. I feel as though I just closed my eyes. I couldn't get enough of Harry last night. Kissing her forehead, I release her so she can roll out of bed, and I follow close behind. She dresses silently as I pull on my boxers and jeans from last night. "I prefer to watch you taking your clothes off than putting them on."

She huffs out a laugh and glances at me. "I could say the same for you."

"Then let's just take them off and climb back into bed. It's still the middle of the night."

"I'm sorry." She steps closer to me, placing her hand over my heart. The heat of her palm sears my bare flesh and I cover her hand with mine to keep her in place. "I should have thought about my early start last night. You go back to bed. I can find my way home. If I don't get moving, I'm going to be late and that'll throw my entire morning schedule out."

I plant a kiss on her tempting lips. "I'll take you home to change, then I'll take you to the café. Once I know you're safely at work, I'll come home and catch a couple of hours of sleep."

"You've already done so much for me, you don't—"

I press my finger to her mouth. "Don't argue with me, Firecracker. It's not negotiable. C'mon. Finish getting dressed and we'll get moving."

The car ride to Harry's apartment building is silent. I think we're both still waking up, well I know *I'm* still half asleep. This has to be the most ridiculous time of the day to be awake. I follow her upstairs and as I look around; I don't like the lack of security here. Anyone could walk off the street and make their way to her front door, which appears flimsy at best. We step through the door and I'm in Harry's space. I'm unsure what I was expecting. Maybe something more feminine. The small space is homey and welcoming, but not girly. Nothing matches, but it all seems to work.

"Take a seat. I won't be long," she throws over her shoulder as she disappears into what I'm assuming is her bedroom. The shower turns on, and I'm tempted to follow her in, but I know she doesn't have time to linger and I don't want a knee in the balls so I spend the time studying the numerous photos she has on display. Most of them feature her with an older woman I'm guessing is her grand-mère; one has her standing in front of her café with a broad smile and her arms stretched out wide, a selfie with Quentin and Judy inside the café, and there are a couple with her grand-mère and an elderly couple, who may be Beverley and Frank. What I notice most is the lack of photographs of her parents and having met them, I understand why that is.

The shower turns off and I peek into her bedroom. The bed's a mess and there's a pile of laundry on a dining chair in the corner. She steps out of the bathroom gloriously naked, and my dick wakes up and presses against the zipper of my jeans. She's in such a hurry to get dressed she's oblivious to my eyes tracing every inch of her silky flesh, her peaked nipples, the dip of her waist, and the curve of her ass.

I need to distract myself. "Do you have an overnight bag?"

She peers at me over her shoulder, her forehead adorably creased in confusion. "Huh?"

"An overnight bag. You know, so you can pack a few days' worth of clothes. You're staying with me."

She spins on her heel to face me directly, panties on, tits exposed. Her hands land on her hips. "Why in the hell would I be staying with you when I have a perfectly good place here that's close to the café?"

I can't help it. I take the two long strides I need to be in her space. My chest brushes the tips of her nipples, and I groan. I want to spread her out on her messy bed and lick every single inch of her beautiful skin, paying special attention to the valley between her legs. I grip her waist and run my thumbs beneath her breasts. She sucks in a sharp breath, and I'm elated that I have such an effect on her. "If you were staying with me, we would have more time to do other things before you get ready for work." I press the bulge trapped behind my zipper against her stomach.

Her eyes widen and her hands move to my hips, her fingers sliding through the belt loops, holding me to her. "Yeah," she says breathily.

"Uh-huh." I rub my nose alongside hers and drift across to

her ear, where I lay a tender kiss. She shivers in response. "Pack a bag."

Once she quickly throws a few things in a bag and grabs her toiletries, I take the bag from her and we head downstairs. Driving to her café in the dark, I check the time. "How late are you?"

She glances at her phone. "Uh, only about fifteen minutes. We haven't done too bad."

"Can I do anything to help?"

She smiles at me, and it's like the dawn breaking through the clouds. "Nah. I'll be okay." She squeezes my thigh. "You probably need more sleep." We pull into the lot behind her café, and I'm pleased to see the motion sensor lights turn on. She turns to me with a furrow between her brows. "I guess I'll see you later?"

I cup her face gently. "Yeah, you'll see me later. I'll come and grab lunch and we'll work things out." She nods and I press my lips to hers in a hungry kiss that's going to have to hold me over until I see her later. Now that I've had her properly, I'm not sure I'll be able to make it through the day without touching her.

She pulls away with a smile. "I really need to go." She cups my cheek. "Thanks for last night and this morning."

"You're welcome." I climb out of my car and jog around to her side to open the door. She presses up on her toes to plant a quick kiss and then steps around me to head inside. I smack her ass playfully, making her jump, and watch her go inside.

I've decided I'm addicted to Harry. I can't stay away from the woman. Every day for the past two weeks, I've stopped by for lunch, taken Harry home, defiled her in every possible way, then curled my body around hers to sleep. Each day we wake tangled together and start the process all over again.

Things at the pub have settled down since I fired Blaze. Callahan's hidden camera had captured him stealing the alcohol, confirming my suspicions. I spoke with Thomas about everything Blaze had done. He didn't think filing a report would achieve anything because the video evidence we had wouldn't be admissible in court, and even though what he did to Harry was intimidating, there wasn't much the police could do about it because he didn't physically harm her. The court system is so swamped that only the worst crimes see the light of day—the system is broken. Having a police officer for a friend comes in handy sometimes.

When I walk into Harry's café a little after one, pride fills me to see how busy it is. She's too busy serving a customer to notice my arrival, so I join the end of the line, waiting patiently for my turn to be served. Studying her without her knowledge, I note that her sparkle's missing today, just like it's been since Beverley passed. I don't think it's noticeable to those who don't know her well, but I can tell she's having a sad day.

I step to the front of the line and as she looks up noticing me, a genuine smile graces her lips, not the pretend one she's been putting on for her customers. "Hey, Firecracker."

Her shoulders drop, and her posture visibly softens. "Hey, you."

I lean over the counter and gesture for her to meet me halfway. She glances around but meets me for a light kiss that quickly evolves into something hotter, something not appropriate for our location or present company. A throat clears nearby and I drag myself away from Harry to find Matthew watching us with a smirk and raised brows. "So, is there something you forgot to tell me?"

Judy breezes out of the kitchen, her eyes catching on the three of us. "What's going on?"

Matthew points to me and Harry, waving his finger between us. "They were making out over the counter."

Harry playfully smacks him with the back of her hand across his stomach. "Such a tattletale."

"You mean, reporter of the facts?" Judy says as she twists toward the kitchen. "Quentin, get out here!"

Harry groans.

Quentin pokes his head around the door frame. "What?"

With a twinkle in her eyes and mischief on her lips, Judy waves her hand between me and Harry. "These two were kissing."

His eyebrows shoot up and he steps out of the kitchen. "Yeah." Judy nods, and his hard gaze locks on me. "What are your intentions with Harry?" he asks as he wipes his hands on a towel.

"Oh my God. We're not in the eighteenth century, Quentin. Next, you'll be asking about his dowry." She turns to me, her eyes full of apology. "I'm so sorry. Please ignore my employees." She glares at each one, but they don't seem fazed. What I love most about this moment is that Harry's fire has returned, even if it's all in good fun.

While they're all chuckling, I blurt, "I'm gonna marry her one day." I'm mystified how we got to this point so quickly, but it seems like the natural next step for us and I have no desire to take my words back.

All laughing ceases instantly and Harry's head snaps around to me. Quentin looks like a proud uncle and Judy looks as though she's ready to burst with happiness.

"Best news ever," Matthew chirps.

"You can't be serious," Harry states.

"One hundred percent, you can take it to the bank, serious, Firecracker." I finish with a wink as her hand lands on her hip.

"Are you telling me or asking me?"

I glance around at her friends, then around the café where everyone seems to be holding their breath. I take Harry's hand and lead her out from behind the counter, then drop to one knee. I didn't come here with this in mind, but it feels right and I'm gonna go with it. I draw in a deep breath, then look up into her stunning green eyes. "Harry, you are the woman of my dreams. From the moment we first met, I couldn't get enough of your fire." She smirks down at me. I'm sure she's remembering that first meeting when I was shocked to discover that Harry was a woman. "So much so that I kept finding excuses to see you and piss you off as much as I possibly could." Snickers sound throughout the space. "I want to be the man to piss you off for the rest of my days, but I also want to be the man who holds your broken pieces together on your bad days, and the man who gets to laugh with you through the good times. I want to be the man who supports you as you succeed and makes you round with my babies. I want to be everything to you and, in return, I want you to be my everything." I hear sighs, but I can't tear my eyes away from Harry to see what's happening around us. "Tell me you'll be my wife."

She lowers her face to mine. Cupping my cheeks, she swipes her lips softly against mine. "I wouldn't want anyone else to piss me off, Finn." Her lips spread in a smile against mine. "I'll be your wife," she whispers.

She presses her lips to mine, and I drag her down so we can properly celebrate that I just proposed and she accepted. Cheers fill the café as I continue to kiss my fiancée, my future. When we pull away, I cup her cheeks. "I can't wait to spend forever getting under your skin and on your nerves."

We both chuckle as her friends and customers swoop in with their congratulations.

Would you like a sneak peek into the future?
Sign up for my newsletter to find out how Harry reacts when she learns
about the secret Finn's been keeping.
https://tinyurl.com/enemykisses-bonus

Are you ready to meet Finn's friend, Max, in **Moonlit Kisses?**
An age-gap workplace romance
A steamy, low-angst, stand-alone contemporary romance about
a workaholic mechanic with a generous heart fighting his
attraction to his assistant, and a younger woman who's down
on her luck but never gives in or gives up.
https://books2read.com/dsj-moonlitkisses

Are you ready to meet Toby Summer in **Second Chance Summer?**
A rock star/single mom second chance romance

A steamy, stand-alone contemporary romance about a
magnetic, protective rock star and a sexy single mom doing her
best to protect her deaf daughter.

https://books2read.com/dsj-2ndchancesummer

pinterest

I put together a Pinterest board for Finn and Harriet's story. If you're
interested, you can check it out here:
https://tinyurl.com/enemykisses-pinterestboard

debra's books

The Summer Twins

Loving Summer | *Kate Summer & Oliver Stone*

Second Chance Summer | *Toby Summer & Cassia Phillips*

The Summer Twins | Complete Series

Spin-off Novella

Loving Roman | *Roman Armstrong & Alice Reed*

Kisses

Stolen Kisses | *Emma Miller & Theo Drivas*

Moonlit Kisses | *Max Stanfield & Molly Lewis*

Unexpected Kisses | *Sarah Stanfield & AJ*

Kisses | Complete Series

Monday Knights | *novellas*

Enemy Kisses | *Finn Brady & Harriet Dubois*

Wicked Kisses | *Lincoln Kingsley & Sophie Chalmers*

Everlasting

Everlasting Love | *Shane Sutton & Violet Jamison*

Everlasting Promises | *Hope Sullivan & Benjamin Taylor*

Everlasting Vows | *Nixon Steele & Abigail Steele*

Debra has a list of her books available on her website.

You can find them here:

https://debrastjamesbooks.com

connect with debra

stalk me

You can stalk me pretty much everywhere!
https://debrastjamesbooks.com/connect/

How about joining my Facebook group?
https://www.facebook.com/groups/DebsBibliomaniacs

newsletter

Join Debra's newsletter to receive important updates before anyone else. Newsletters will be sent once a month unless something exciting is happening.
https://debrastjamesbooks.com/newsletter/

thank you

Thank you so much for reading Finn and Harriet's story. When I was invited to write an enemies-to-lovers story for an anthology to raise funds for Suicide Prevention, I jumped at the chance to support a worthy cause, then spent the next several months wondering how to make two people who hate each other, fall in love. Finn and Harry were so much fun to write with their banter and Finn's innuendos.

As always, I would like to thank Mr. St James and our two sons for their support and patience with me. My writing takes a lot of my time away from my family and their understanding and support is always appreciated.

To my beta readers, Rachel, Kelly, and Wendy, thank you for your invaluable feedback. I'd also like to shout out to Rachel's hubby for his contributions in the background. :)

To my online support network, you were there for me on the days when I doubted myself. Ladies, you are so very important to me. I'm grateful we connected and I can call you my friends.

To you, the reader. Thank you for taking a chance on me; for reading my book. I truly do appreciate your time. If you've enjoyed reading about Finn and Harriet, I'd love to hear from you.

about the author

Debra St James is an author of spicy, slow-burn contemporary romance that features cinnamon roll heroes who listen to their women's hearts and their words. She takes her time to weave a detailed tapestry of genuine characters, real-life struggles, love, and romance to create engaging stories that will have you so immersed in the story that you'll never want to leave. Her stories are always guaranteed to take you on an emotional journey that ultimately ends with a HEA!

Debra loves to read romance. Her family often finds her with her nose stuck in her iPad, swooning over her latest book boyfriend. She writes part-time from her Perth home, which she shares with Mr St James and their two sons, whose antics often make her roll her eyes and laugh in equal measure.

Writing a novel had never been on her radar. One morning, she was enjoying a coffee by the river and a story sprouted, seemingly from nowhere. At 51, she pulled up the Pages app on her phone and began to type, giving life to her debut, *Loving Summer*.

The rest, as they say, is history!

Debra xo

amazon.com/author/debrastjames

facebook.com/debra.stjames.books

instagram.com/debrastjames_books

bookbub.com/authors/debra-st-james

goodreads.com/debrastjames

pinterest.com/debrastjamesbooks

www.ingramcontent.com/pod-product-compliance
Lightning Source LLC
Chambersburg PA
CBHW071923130726
47909CB00014B/2533